SWORDS OF DESTINY

Sue Vincent

When Rhea Marchant heads north to the wild and beautiful landscapes of the Yorkshire Dales, she is plunged into an adventure that will span the worlds. She sees herself as no more than ordinary; yet it seems the strange old man who is her new employer sees something more than a middle aged widow with a passion for paint.

As his true identity is revealed and ancient powers wake, the very earth beneath their feet reveals its hidden life as Rhea and her new companions are guided by the ancient Keeper in search of artefacts of arcane power.

With the aid of the Old Ones and the merry immortal Heilyn, the company seek the elemental weapons that will help restore hope to an unbalanced world at the dawn of a new era.

Second Edition

First published 2013 as Sword of Destiny

ISBN: 978-1-910478-26-4

SWORDS OF DESTINY

SUE VINCENT

Always, Love

CONTENTS

Chapter One

RHEA

Taking a deep breath, Rhea knocked on the door of room twenty - three, clutching the red leather portfolio containing the images which, she hoped, would be the key to a new beginning. The door was opened by an old gentleman with a decided twinkle in his peat brown eyes.

"Mrs Marchant? Good afternoon. . Please, do come in. I am Professor Ambrose." Rhea took the proffered hand and allowed herself to be drawn into the small sitting room. "I hope you don't mind, but I've taken the liberty of having tea sent up."

Rhea found herself seated in one of the chintz covered armchairs, minus her overcoat and portfolio.

"Would you like to pour? It is a rare pleasure to have a pretty young woman to tea." Rhea looked up, with a rueful smile.

"Neither pretty nor very young these days, I'm afraid," she replied.

"My dear, you are young from my perspective," said the old gentleman, "and beauty is something each of us is free to seek wherever we wish. You, as an artist, will see much beauty in the world that others will overlook. The dance of light on water, the rainbow imprisoned in a dew drop... we all look, but few have the soul to *see*." The Professor held Rhea's gaze as if he would see into her very soul and for a fleeting moment Rhea imagined that she stood naked and unafraid in a vast cavern of light. "That is why I need an artist, not a photographer, to illustrate my work. Now, shall we?" he asked, indicating the portfolio.

Rhea spread the delicate watercolour landscapes across the table. In silence the Professor examined her work, lingering over two rather fanciful impressions that Rhea had almost left at home.

"What are these?"

"I had a dream a few nights ago," Rhea explained. "I tried to paint it."

Professor Ambrose smiled, but made no comment on the paintings.

"The pay would be minimal I'm afraid, but there is a small cottage available, a studio and all the materials you can use. It is a very beautiful part of England but we are fairly remote at Stone Lodge. In addition to detailed illustrations of specific sites, I would like you to be able to capture something of the spirit of the moors in your work, so you could paint to your heart's content. Well, that's my side of the story, Mrs Marchant. Perhaps you can tell me a little about yourself?" The Professor leaned back in the big armchair and gestured for Rhea to begin.

"What can I tell you? I will be forty-two this year. I'm a widow, my husband died three years ago in a road accident. I have a daughter, Anna, who is travelling with two friends and will be gone until Spring. At present I have a small flat in Bicester and I work as a receptionist which pays enough to keep me in paint." Rhea suddenly smiled for the first time and her face did indeed become young and pretty.

"I have no formal training. I only began to paint after I lost Michael. It was just an escape, something to fill the time, but it sort of took over and then friends began to offer to buy my pictures." The words were tumbling out in a rush and the old man's smile widened.

"Of course, I couldn't sell them to people I care about, but I did place a few with a local craft shop and those went too. I never expected to be able to earn a living by painting, so I was thrilled when you asked me here for an interview."

"But my dear Mrs Marchant, I am afraid there has been a slight misunderstanding," interrupted the Professor. Rhea's heart sank. "Having seen the copies of your work which you were kind enough to send me, I asked you here today not for an interview, but to offer you the position! I assure you I have seen no one else whose work will suit me as much as yours. What do you say, would you consider working for an eccentric Professor in the wilds of Yorkshire?"

"Oh yes, please. I would love to!"

"Wonderful! The cottage is all ready for you. When can you start?"

For the next half an hour, details were discussed, travel arranged and dates fixed. Professor Ambrose was studying the early history of the area commonly known as Ilkley Moor, although its real name was Rombald's Moor, "after the giant who sleeps there," he explained.

Rhea's task would be to illustrate the book he was preparing and help with organising the work in progress. The Professor... "call me Ambrose, my dear, as I have every intention of using your own lovely name"... wished to produce a work which not only breathed life into history but could also capture the imagination through myth and legend retold.

When all had been decided, Rhea began to collect the scattered paintings. Ambrose again picked up the dreamscapes and quietly studied the misty images.

"One last thing before you leave, Rhea. In your dream, did you choose to bathe in the Fountain?"

Rhea turned, the sheaf of paper betraying her trembling hands. Seconds ticked away as she considered a question that the old gentleman should not have been able to ask.

This was her dream, she had told no-one about it. With Anna away, there was no-one to tell. Nor would words have conveyed the menace of the dream or the afterglow of hope that had followed in its wake. Her tormentor waited for her reply, his eyes full of kindness and understanding. And knowledge, Rhea realised.

"How can you... what do you know of the fountain?"

"Let us say that having lived so long I can see a little deeper than most," the Professor replied. "Tell me about your dream."

Rhea sat back and closed her eyes, hands clasped and only the rapid pulse at the base of her throat betraying her emotion.

"I was in a strange town and I was searching for someone. I don't know who. Someone I cared for very much. But I wasn't alone. Oh, the town was deserted, but I wasn't alone. There were two figures, men perhaps, it was hard to be certain.

"They were serene and beautiful, but their faces were immobile, without expression. Their hair was long and their robes were colourless rather than white. There was something very odd about them, neither their hair nor their clothing seemed to move and they felt menacing, though not evil. It's hard to explain."

"Go on, my dear, I understand."

"They were herding me out of town, along a cliff top. I had no choice but to go where they willed, though no word was spoken and they never came close enough to touch. The path led down towards a bay. The sea, sand and cliffs were all of that same colourless hue. The beach was full of people, pale-clad and aimless, alive, but vague. There was nowhere to go, no escape from the beach, but they seemed not to care or even notice.

"The two Figures stopped halfway down the cliff path. There was a white tree beside a pool of clear water. No-one spoke and yet I was told, somehow, that this was the Fountain of Forgetfulness and I should bathe in it to wash away all the pain of my loss, all the old heartaches and suffering in my life. I had only to bathe and all the hurt would be forgotten. At the same time I was shown, like a slow motion picture that tore at my heart, all the things in my life I would love to forget. Wounds were laid bare in my soul and I was given the chance to wipe the slate clean. And I so wanted to forget the pain, to stop missing Mike in the night, to have no memory of tears."

"Did you bathe in the Fountain?"

"No." Rhea took a deep breath. "To forget the hurt would be to deny the happiness and forget the lessons learned through the pain. To forget would have made me one of the colourless people, like those on the beach, lost and denying my own humanity. No, I chose to remain myself; whole, imperfect and human."

Rhea opened her eyes as she felt a soothing touch on her hair and a crisp white handkerchief appeared in front of her eyes.

"My dear Rhea, I knew I had made a good choice in you, but now I know I have made the right one. In time you will understand more than you do just now, I promise you. You have shown much courage and I will be proud to have you work with me. You have chosen life over mindless oblivion and that choice is its own reward. You are a remarkable woman. Now, dry your eyes and I promise not to ask any more awkward questions," again, the gentle chuckle, "I don't want you to run away."

Rhea blew her nose in a business-like way on the borrowed handkerchief and smiled.

"Oh no, Professor Ambrose, I shan't run away."

"No, my dear," replied the old gentleman, "I don't believe you will."

Chapter Two

ROMBALD'S MOOR

Rhea opened her eyes, blinking at the early morning sun which streamed through a chink in the curtains. She had fallen into bed last night after dumping her bags in the hall. She had barely been sufficiently awake to examine her new home but the immediate impression had been one of welcoming comfort. The clock on the bedside table was ticking away the last few seconds before seven o'clock as Rhea threw back the heavy eiderdown and slid reluctantly out of bed.

The cottage was a window on the past. Whitewashed walls of rough plaster gave the bedroom the illusion of space and the glow of burnished oak gave it warmth. The scent of lavender and beeswax followed Rhea into the sitting room where it mingled with the perfume of a large vase of roses. A small card bade her welcome and invited her to breakfast with the Professor at eight. The window looked out over a stone wall, across a narrow road to the moor she was to paint. The view was all bleak stone and bracken, a few sheep and neither tree nor building in sight. Rhea understood why many found this land empty and forbidding, but standing there, watching a solitary skylark on its erratic flight, Rhea Marchant fell in love.

A little while later, showered and groomed in the tiny, but surprisingly modern bathroom, Rhea crossed the grounds to Stone Lodge.

The house was a long, low building of the local sandstone which seemed to fit naturally into the landscape. The front door was open to the morning chill, so Rhea knocked and walked into the hall. The clattering of pans led her towards the kitchen where breakfast was being prepared by a middle aged lady of ample girth.

"Good morning," said Rhea, "Professor Ambrose asked me to come over." The woman turned at the sound of Rhea's voice to reveal a vast expanse of paisley pinafore.

"You'll be Mrs Marchant then. Welcome to the Lodge. I'm Mrs Long, the housekeeper here. Anything you need, ask me. No use asking the Professor, not a practical bone in his body, that one. Stuck in his books, he'd forget to eat if he wasn't reminded. Now if you'll bide a moment, I'll take you through to the dining room." As she spoke, Mrs Long deposited several sausages and a pile of bacon in a serving dish. "Could you take the tea? Thank you. Follow me"

Rhea grabbed the teapot as the housekeeper hefted a laden tray and set off down the corridor, ramrod straight, and with unexpected speed. She caught up as Mrs Long reached the dining room and was directed to sit.

"You may as well start without him, he'll be in shortly I expect." She gave Rhea an appraising stare, taking in the slim figure and pale complexion.

"You will be eating a Christian breakfast I take it?" Rhea, feeling like a schoolgirl again, stifled a grin and nodded meekly. "I'll leave a packed lunch on the hall table for you. No doubt you'll be off exploring later." Mrs Long swept out of the room carrying an assortment of empty trays and leaving in her wake a table laden with food in chafing dishes.

Four places were laid and Rhea was speculating on the identity of the other guests when the door was flung open by a pair of boisterous collies who flopped down beside the hearth, tongues lolling. They were followed a few moments later by a young man of medium build in jeans, a misshapen sweater and stockinged feet. One toe peeped through the thick sock to complete the picture. He paused on the threshold and looked at Rhea in rueful dismay.

"Oh lord, I forgot we had company this morning," the young man crossed the room and held out a grubby hand to Rhea. "I'm Jamie Dixon; I'm helping Professor Ambrose with his research. Look, I'll be back in a minute or two but it won't do to let the sergeant major catch me coming in to eat dressed like this."

"Then you should make less noise coming in, Mr Jamie," said Mrs Long following him into the room with a fresh regiment of toast in her hands. Jamie took the toast rack from her and planted a kiss on her cheek, a gesture which elicited a snort from the housekeeper.

"Have you met our Sissie yet? She bullies us all and runs the Lodge with absolute efficiency. She also makes the most wonderful scones."

"Well someone needs to look after you all, that's for certain," responded the housekeeper, eyeing the protruding toe, "and don't think you're too old to have your backside tanned for your cheek, young man," she added as she left. "The scones are behind the teapot and you may as well get on with it before they get cold."

Rhea answered the impish gleam in Jamie's eyes with amusement. The obvious affection in which the two protagonists held each other boded well for the start of her new job and much of her nervousness had dissipated with the light-hearted exchange.

Generously applying butter to the still steaming scones, Jamie asked Rhea how she liked the cottage, explaining that he himself occupied a room in the Lodge. No, he assured her, she hadn't ousted him from the cottage, he much preferred to stay at the house where Sissie Long spoiled and scolded him daily.

"Would you like me to show you the stone circle later? Unless the Prof has anything else in mind, of course."

"That would be wonderful! I didn't know there was one. I've studied the maps and I'm sure I'd have seen it marked."

"No, it's only shown on the more detailed survey maps, but in fact there are at least three, plus the Doubler stones and the Swastika stone at the other end of the moor. There are several very interesting sites within easy walking distance and they all seem to be overlooked by the tourists and guidebooks. The locals are the best source of information, though they don't take kindly to anything or anyone who attempts to interfere with their moor." Jamie finished his second scone and helped himself to bacon and eggs. "But if we are to work together, I can't go on calling you Mrs Marchant. What is your first name?" The answer came from the Professor who entered the room with another man at his side.

"She is named for the daughter of the oldest goddess, the earth, who became the mother of gods, she is called Rhea. Though whether you should be allowed the chance to take more liberties then you already have this morning is debatable," added the old gentleman, eyeing the depleted batch of scones in mock severity. "My dear, may I introduce to you our friend and neighbour, Alec Graham. He was kind enough to bring some supplies for your studio back from Leeds yesterday. They are still in his car so after we have eaten you might like to have a look and see if we've forgotten anything."

Alec took Rhea's outstretched hand.

"Welcome to Yorkshire. I hope you will enjoy your stay here and not find the place too quiet for you. Leeds and Bradford are lively enough and only a few miles down the road, but you'll find Ilkley and Burley are quiet little places."

Rhea had the distinct impression that he disapproved of her in some way and didn't expect her to settle here. The coolly formal greeting made her hackles rise and she hoped Alec Graham was not a frequent visitor at the Lodge.

"I like the quiet and the countryside here appeals to me far more than the manicured fields of the south. I'm sure I'll be very happy here."

"Well," said the Professor, deftly confiscating the jam pot from Jamie, "shall we eat?"

After breakfast, Rhea was escorted to the studio the Professor had provided for her. It was housed in the converted stables and large windows in the roof, supplemented by daylight bulbs, provided ample illumination. A standing easel and sloping table occupied the centre of the floor; two walls were lined with shelving while the third was fitted with a sink, kettle and 'fridge. The Professor beamed in appreciation of her obvious pleasure.

"I think we've remembered everything, but Alec has offered to pick up anything we've overlooked." Rhea, avidly examining the contents of the shelves, laughed outright.

"You can't possibly have forgotten anything! There are materials here I've never even tried before!" There were also piles of paper, sketch books, canvases and boards, plus a small collection of books about the area and its history and a lightweight sketching easel. "It's wonderful, Professor! Thank you, I feel like a child at Christmas!"

"This is the last box," said Alec, placing his cargo on the draining board. "I'd better be going, Ambrose, I'm having lunch with Elizabeth and I'll have to change before I go. I'll see you around seven tonight. Nice to have met you, Mrs Marchant." Alec strode out of the studio before Rhea had chance to reply.

No, she thought, he definitely didn't like her, though she could not imagine what she had said or done to warrant such blatant disapproval. He was very cold, almost hostile.

"Don't worry about Alec, my dear," chuckled the Professor, noting her expression of annoyance. "He is a little difficult to get to know, but it is well worth the effort. It was he who stocked the studio for you, he knows a little about artists' needs, you see. It may help if I tell you that he was engaged to be married to a young painter some years ago. He worshipped her with all the passion of youth, but a contract in New York seemed a better proposition to her than the future Alec was offering." The old gentleman named one of the more outrageous modern artists. "She made quite a name for herself, but it hurt Alec deeply. Personally, from the little I know of the lady, I think Alec had a lucky escape, but logic doesn't mend hearts and Alec will have to work that out for himself one day." Rhea privately thought that for Alec to judge her on the strength of past heartache was more than a little unfair. She would probably have said so had not Jamie arrived, armed with supplies of tea and coffee for the studio, sent by the redoubtable Mrs Long.

"I have been instructed to tell you that there is a fruitcake in the tin which will keep for a week or so if you remember to put the lid on tightly. The sergeant major must think you need looking after too."

"I believe it is part of the Yorkshire character to make people feel welcome by feeding them," said the Professor. "I hope you will be with us for a long time and you will see for yourself that whenever you are invited into someone's home here, their first thought will be to put the kettle on to boil. They're a very hospitable people."

"You said 'they'... you're not a Yorkshireman yourself then?" asked Rhea.

"No, child. My roots are in Wales if they are anywhere, though I have travelled very far in my lifetime, so that my home is wherever I have need to be." Rhea thought this reply a little strange, but there was going to be plenty of time to learn more about her new companions. "Now, I have no doubt you would like to have a good look around your studio. Why don't you spend half an hour or so in here while I go through a few things with Jamie, then you might like to let him take you out onto the moor."

"Just come up to the Lodge when you're ready," said Jamie, 'We'll grab a packed lunch and go up to the circle. Bring a sketchbook!"

The two men left and Rhea was free to rummage among the selection of paints and books. She chose two soft graphite pencils and a range of watercolours to fit the pocket sized field box and filled its tiny water bottle. Two sable brushes and a wad of tissue were added to the pile along with a spiral bound pad of heavy paper. These she gathered up and took back to the cottage, where she donned walking boots and a duffle coat with pockets large enough to take all she needed.

Rhea met Jamie at the door of the Lodge. He was carrying a small rucksack in which, he informed her, the sergeant major had packed field rations for the day and the two set off for Rhea's first look at the moorland she was to capture in paint.

"A few rules for the moors," said Jamie. "Shut any gates, ignore the sheep and always tell someone where you're going if you come up here alone. You can always take the dogs for company when they have got to know you . They know better than to chase the sheep up here, which is more than can be said of some of the tourists."

"Do you get many tourists here?"

"Lord yes, in summer there are hundreds of them, though most stick to the path across the front of the moor, where we will be going today. T Cow and Calf are always busy with rock climbers. There's a car park and a decent hotel there too."

While they talked, they had crossed the grounds of the Lodge which, apart from a flower border beneath the windows, looked like an extension of the moor. A cattle grid guarded the gate from the intrusion of sheep and after that it was only a matter of crossing the lane to reach the moor itself.

Rhea was immediately struck by the change in atmosphere as they began to climb. The ground underfoot was springy with last year's bracken and the whole place seemed ancient and remote from the modern world.

The few sheep grazing nearby treated them with utter indifference as they made their way to the worn path which Jamie said was their easiest way to reach their destination. At the top of the hill there was a haphazard pile of small rocks. Jamie looked around for a suitable stone which he added to the others.

"This is a cairn. When Ambrose first brought me up here he said they are thought to be way markers for shepherds. There are few of those these days though and they would hardly need a marker this close to the road. The cairns must date back centuries and yet, despite being redundant for the last couple of hundred years, they still stand. I like the feeling of continuity. I will always add to a cairn when I pass one."

Jamie seemed a little embarrassed by his confession but Rhea knew exactly what he meant as she also found a stone and laid it on the mound with a strange, almost reverent feeling. As if, she thought, that by her action she had somehow made a commitment to the land. The two shared a smile before continuing along the uneven track.

Following the top of the ridge, the high moor to their left stretched back to the horizon. On their right, the land sloped down to the river before climbing to the peaks on the other side of the valley. Small towns and villages followed the course of the Wharfe and Jamie pointed out their own village and the nearby town of Ilkley. The hills on the other side of the valley had a more lived in look, thought Rhea. Only the peaks still retained their wildness. Jamie told her the highest peak they could see from here was called Simon's Seat, but couldn't tell her why.

"Except," he said, "that local legend says that Druids worshipped there who were associated with Simon Magus, the Samaritan magician. And this version of him claimed to have been one of the three Wise Men.

"Ambrose thinks it may once have been Solomon's Seat, but we're still working on it," he explained. They scrambled down a rocky slope and sat for a while beside a stream.

"There's a dig just behind that rise. Nothing spectacular, but they have found an early Iron Age settlement. You get a good view of the Cow and Calf from the top of the next rise. That seems to have been in use as a natural fortress since the Stone Age. There is a sort of quarry behind it and it's not uncommon to find flint tools there still. There are hundreds of ancient rock carvings up here too. Come on, there's plenty to see over the next hill."

Rhea climbed to her feet and followed the young man up the steep slope. Jamie reached back to help her over the last boulders at the top.

"Look over there." Jamie indicated a rocky outcrop jutting out over the top of the cliff. "Giant Rombald." Rhea saw the craggy profile of a head in the formation of rocks. "It's even more impressive from the other side, you'll see."

As they walked Jamie recounted some of the legends associated with the giant. "Other stories say he is a druid who was imprisoned here by magic, but it has been a sacred place since before the druids came to power." They reached the stone and Rhea ran her hand over the weathered surface, feeling the texture of the lichen encrusted rock. "The depressions and lines cut into the surface are cup and ring marks. No one knows for certain what they mean or how far back they go. We believe they have some kind of ritual significance, probably to do with the sun."

"How old are they?"

"Certainly Iron Age, possibly earlier. They are at all the sacred sites on the moor, and you can find them all over Britain. There are other carvings up here too, more, I think, than anywhere else in England. You'll see them all at some point," promised Jamie. "The locals call this a rocking stone. You can see the giant's hair is a separate slab, balanced on top of the head."

Jamie made a show of trying to move the massive block. It didn't move at all. Rhea was hardly surprised given its size and the accretion of soil and pebbles under the rim.

"I still try," he laughed. "The legends say that only an honest man will move the stone. The locals add that this explains why no true Yorkshireman ever will!" Rhea was puzzled. "You have heard the Yorkshire Tyke's motto"

"I'm afraid not."

"You still see it on souvenirs all over the county. We are proud of our traditions here you know. It goes:

'See all, hear all, say nowt.

Eyt all, sup all, pay nowt.

An if tha' does owt for nowt

Allus do it for thi'sen.'"

Rhea burst out laughing at Jamie's rendition in broadest Yorkshire dialect. It took some minutes before she calmed down enough to apologise to Jamie, who had affected a pose of affronted dignity. Then she got out her pad and began a swift sketch of the rocking stone.

"Your motto seems to be a complete contradiction of the people I've met since I've been here," said Rhea.

"Thank you, dear lady." Jamie bowed, in a fair imitation of the Professor. He watched the image take on form and depth as she sketched. "We're not a bad lot on the whole."

A few minutes later the sketches were complete and they moved on. "We go down to another stream, and then back up and we're at the stone circle. Don't expect Stonehenge, but there's something special about it for me."

"You really love his place don't you, Jamie?" Rhea could hear it in the tone of his voice and see it in his face.

"Yes, I do. The place, the people and the family I have found here," he replied. "The Prof has given me far more than just a room and a job. He has given me a home." The faraway look in his eyes told Rhea that she was not the only one with a story of loss in her life and her heart went out to the young man. She laid her hand on his arm in a quick gesture of understanding and unspoken empathy.

"How old are you, Jamie?

"Twenty-three."

"My daughter is twenty-one," said Rhea and started down the path to the stream.

Chapter Three

PROFESSOR AMBROSE

"Rhea, Rhea! Are you okay?" Jamie's voice broke through the mist and Rhea grasped at the lifeline it offered. She fought her way back to reality and found herself on her knees before the altar stone. "Rhea, look at me, are you okay? Gods, but you scared me." Jamie's voice was low and worried. Rhea opened her eyes and fought to focus on his face, his usual expression of levity replaced by one of concern. "What happened? One moment you were fine, then you cried out and you lost it somehow."

"I'm not sure. I must have blacked out for a moment I suppose. I'll be fine in a minute." Rhea adjusted her position so she could lean against the stone. "Is there any coffee in that rucksack?" Jamie dived in the bag and found the flask Mrs Long had provided. He filled a cup and handed it to Rhea.

"You were gone for more than a moment, you know," he said quietly. "You must have been out for at least ten minutes." Rhea choked on her coffee and stared at him in disbelief. "What happened?"

Jamie had shown her the double circle of small boulders and made her pace out the distances between them to see for herself that they had to have been placed there by human hands. She had duly admitted that the rocking stone was a far more convincing giant from here and had listened to the explanation that the rising sun struck first the rocking stone, or Hele Stone, then the altar, at dawn on Midsummer's Day. Jamie had taken great delight in pointing out a strip of lighter vegetation that ran from the altar stone to the edge of the moor which, he insisted, marked an ancient trough, cut into the ground to carry the blood from those sacrificed on the stone. He had embellished the tale with gruesome and fictitious detail until Rhea had suggested they have lunch.

Having thoroughly disgusted the young man with her lack of response to the gory tale, she had relented and agreed that they should at least examine the altar before eating. This was the only obviously impressive thing about the circle and even this would have been passed by most people without a second glance.

It was a large rock, perhaps ten feet long and six feet high, shaped almost exactly like a couch and known locally as the Haystack. However, Jamie had saved the best for last, for cut into the stone were definite figures. They were simple stick men, such as a child might draw, but with a halo-like circle around their heads. The Sun God. Rhea had felt drawn to them, an almost living link with the circle's past that had felt the wind since before time was counted.

"I don't really know," replied Rhea. "I remember looking at the carvings, trying to understand them a little better. I put my hands out to trace the figures and as I touched the rock I felt something like an electric shock." She closed her eyes against the ache in her temples. Whirling light and colour, a voice and a presence. "No I must have been dreaming." Rhea shook her head to dispel the lingering images and forced a tremulous smile. "I'm sorry, Jamie, I must have given you a real fright, but honestly, I don't make a habit of this kind of thing, I promise!"

Jamie too had begun to recover and smiled back.

"Just as well, if you're thinking of coming up here on your own." He glanced at his watch and walked to the edge of the circle, looking down at the Cow and Calf below. "If you really do feel better then perhaps we should start down now."

"I'd like to do a few initial sketches first, if you don't mind. There's no hurry is there? I'll be fine in a little while." Jamie looked a little guilty.

"Well, when I couldn't rouse you, I had visions of trying to carry you down from the moor on my own," he confessed, taking a mobile phone out of his pocket by way of explanation. "So I, er, called the cavalry."

"What?"

"Well, actually, I called the Prof and he took it from there. Alec is on his way and if you really are feeling better, it would be easier to go down and meet him." Rhea closed her eyes again picturing the scene and acutely embarrassed. "We can see the car park from here so we shan't miss him." Rhea groaned, but drained her cup and got to her feet.

Jamie was by Rhea's side every step of the way down, ready with a steadying hand over the uneven ground in spite of her protestations. His concern touched Rhea and, in truth, she still felt unstable and there was a nagging ache behind her eyes. Again she found herself wondering about Jamie's own story, but she knew too little to draw any conclusions. Something, or someone, had hurt the young man, she felt, but she wasn't about to re-open any old wounds but prying uninvited. She was also trying to make sense of what had happened and something was tugging at her memory, something she couldn't quite bring into focus.

Jamie kept up a light conversation, teaching her how to identify the many boggy patches by seeking out the distinctive short reeds.

"It's quite dry just now, though you would still get muddy feet, but be careful if you come up here after rain."

The two were about a hundred yards from the final drop to the car park when Alec crested the rise. Rhea watched him scan the moor and make his way swiftly towards them. Jamie waved, rather unnecessarily, thought Rhea grimly, to attract his attention. She was dreading this encounter, given Alec's already apparent disapproval.

Jamie had explained that Alec, a great friend of the Professor and frequent visitor to the Lodge, lived a mile farther down the road towards Burley. He had inherited a small publishing business from his father. He had worked hard and turned it into a successful venture which he had quit five years ago. He now owned a small bookshop in Leeds, run by his younger sister, Sabrina. Rhea, barely listening, was very sure he would not be pleased at having his lunch date with the unknown Elizabeth interrupted for what was, essentially, a false alarm.

"Ah, the knight in shining armour," quipped Jamie, "I'm glad the Prof caught you, Alec."

"I'm just sorry you were dragged up here on a wild goose chase," Rhea apologised, "there was no need to disturb you." Alec eyes raked her slight form.

"I see."

"Yes, Rhea says she's fine, thank goodness," said Jamie. "It's me that's in need of a stiff drink. She frightened the life out of me up there!"

"Ambrose rang me at Elizabeth's. All he said was that Mrs Marchant had fainted and you were concerned. What actually happened?" Jamie filled in the details for Alec as they made their way to the car.

"…she went out, I don't think it was a faint," the younger man explained. Alec shot him a questioning glance. Rhea had noticed that though Alec wasted few words, his eyes spoke volumes. "I don't know how to describe it, she was unconscious didn't respond to me at all, yet she stayed kneeling upright for the whole ten minutes, mumbling something. No, I don't know what she was saying, something about the Professor, I think. Do you remember, Rhea?" She shook her head and immediately regretted doing so. A stab of pain behind her eyes took her by surprise and she caught her breath. Without a word, Alec picked her up and carried her the rest of the way to the car. He threw the keys to Jamie.

"Here, you drive, I'll sit in the back with Mrs Marchant, she looks dreadful." In fact, Rhea now felt so nauseous that she didn't even react to the uncomplimentary remark. With surprising care, Alec fastened her seat belt and climbed in beside her.

"I'm sorry, Alec." A single tear escaped Rhea's control and Alec watched as it ran down her cheek. There was something in the quiet restraint that touched him, he wanted to offer some kind of comfort but felt he had lost the knack of dealing with women, if indeed he had ever had it, he admitted ruefully. Conscious of his cool reception of Rhea, he didn't know if she would accept anything from him at all.

Although the walk across the moor had taken three hours, Rhea was glad that the drive back took only a few minutes. Jamie drove as slowly as he could over the cattle grid but the jarring was almost more than Rhea could bear. Her head was pounding and Alec met with no resistance as he helped her from the car.

Once again Rhea found herself in Alec's arms as he carried her into the cottage and laid her on the bed. Jamie had preceded them, opening doors and closing the curtains. Alec sent him to find a bowl and flannel while he removed Rhea's coat and boots.

"Thanks Jamie, now can you let Ambrose know how things are? I'll stay here till you get back."

Alec sat on the edge of the bed, looking down at his charge. There was nothing remarkable about the face he now had leisure to study. It was attractive, not beautiful; fine lines around the eyes the only blemish to the skin. The long, brown lashes curled against the cheek echoed the colour of her hair. In a crowd she would pass unnoticed "…unless she looked at you," he thought, for the brown eyes were large and clear, their gaze honest and direct.

Alec would have been surprised to know how much comfort Rhea derived from his presence. The calm voice was reassuring and the feel of his arms around her as he carried her had been a balm to the lonely ache she had felt since Mike's death.

That loneliness was a private thing, something she had not been able to talk about with Anna or the well-meaning friends who thought they understood her grief. It was a physical pain, an amputation of the soul. It wasn't just Mike that she missed, she had realised, she also missed simple human contact. To spend twenty three years living with someone and then to find oneself alone. To be able to reach out and touch someone in the night, a hand to hold, a shoulder to cry on, laughter to share; all the silly things which sounded so small and which hurt so much once gone.

There had been a time last summer when she had felt the overwhelming urge to reach out and touch people in the street, total strangers except in their shared humanity. It was an urge she had quickly suppressed. Conscious of her own vulnerability, Rhea had gently repulsed the occasional invitations she had received. Even though Alec disliked her, it was his touch which had caused her tears.

Rhea was also grateful for the competent manner in which he handled the bowl for the next few minutes. Alec had watched the colour drain from her face and noted the beads of sweat forming on her skin. The bowl was already there when it was needed and swiftly disposed of when the wave of nausea had passed. He had held her throughout and wiped her face with a tenderness that took them both by surprise, then laying her back against the pillows, he sat in silence, his thumb stroking the back of the hand that was held in his.

Ambrose found them thus a few minutes later and the worried frown eased to a private smile. He beckoned Alec from the room and Rhea drifted to sleep listening to their muted voices.

It was almost dark when Rhea awoke. A chink of light showed around the door to the sitting room and someone had covered her with the eiderdown while she slept. She sat up gingerly and found, to her relief that the pain and nausea had gone. The sound of movement must have carried to the next room and the door opened on the portly silhouette of the Professor.

"I see you are awake, child. How do you feel?"

"Drained and ridiculous," replied Rhea, "but otherwise quite well." She swung her legs off the bed and stood experimentally. "In fact, I'm hungry. Yes, I really do feel much better."

"Good, then why don't you go and have a shower and freshen up a little and I'll organise some food. Then, if you feel up to it, I think we should talk."

Ten minutes later she emerged looking and feeling much more like herself, with unruly curls clinging damply to her forehead and clad in a long housecoat of deep green. Mrs Long was setting a place for her at the small round table.

"There's chicken soup, rolls and some apple pie I rescued from Mr Jamie," she indicated. "The Professor can make the tea before he leaves you in peace." This with an admonitory look at Ambrose, who was shooing her towards the door.

"Yes, yes, I'll look after her, Mrs Long. I promise I won't keep her up late. I'll even bring the tray back and wash the dishes."

"You'll do no such thing! Just leave the tray in the kitchen and I'll deal with it in the morning. Goodnight, Miss Rhea. I hope you sleep well." With a final glare at her employer Mrs Long stepped out into the night.

Professor Ambrose grinned at Rhea.

"I'll go and make tea." Rhea smiled back and turned her attention to the dishes on the table, while the rattle of china from the kitchen bore witness to the old gentleman's obedience.

The tea tray was brought in just as Rhea finished the last morsel of pie. She could understand why Jamie had wanted to monopolise it, the pastry was perfect. The Professor set the tray down on the coffee table and invited Rhea to come and sit beside him on the sofa.

"Now, child, Alec and Jamie have told me what actually happened this afternoon and as I said, I have an idea what may have caused it. What I do need to hear, though, is what you remember." He took Rhea's hand in his and sat a moment contemplating the contrast between the two: the one smooth, square and practical, the other gnarled as old bark. As always, he prayed to all the gods that he was right in what he was about to do. "Why don't you tell me all about it?"

Rhea sat back and closed her eyes in her typical attitude of concentration, trying to recall the fleeting chiaroscuro which flickered on the edge of memory. An impression began to coalesce of bright forms holding aloft slender blades. In wonder, Rhea tried to find a way to describe the incredible images replaying before her imagination's eyes. Slowly, the words formed by themselves until they were spilling out in a disjointed torrent.

"...and the swords must be found and held by their bearers lest the darkness find a way into the heart of man. Ask the waters to grant guidance and tell the ancient Keeper of Light that it is time to join battle for the next age."

Rhea sighed and opened her eyes wide. The Professor was staring into some unseen distance with an expression of pain and resignation.

"Okay, Professor Ambrose, please can you tell me what all of this means?"

"Yes, child, I'm afraid I can, although whether you believe me or think me senile is a different matter altogether. How credulous are you feeling?"

Rhea appreciated the return of his rich chuckle and responded with a smile, "Try me."

"Very well. I shall start by saying that I have been waiting for this summons for a long time. A very long time. Nor is it the first occasion when the call has been mine to answer. Despite the legends, I am still human and can make mistakes and last time I was called, I failed to find the Champions of

Light in time to avert the catastrophe that was brewing in Europe. The consequences of that failure have haunted me ever since. So many deaths, so much human misery.

"Once the moment had passed, I was powerless to prevent what happened. I could only work behind the scenes to help heal the wounds and mend the rifts, always awaiting the message that would one day come.

"Now the world is lunging toward disaster again. On the material plane the signs are there for anyone with the meanest intelligence to read. On the inner planes there are also signs for those of us who know how to read them. The gravest errors of history are being repeated in an endless cycle.

"My task will be to break that cycle of events and give mankind a chance to take a new direction. The final summons was given today and you were the messenger. I am sorry you were so badly affected; I had not expected the stones to speak to you in that way and was caught off guard. However, if you will let me help you, I can teach you how to deal with these things."

Rhea did not know what to make of all this. She did know she had an awful lot of questions.

"What was this catastrophe, Professor? What were you supposed to do? And who are you?" The old gentleman stood and began pacing the length of the small room.

"This is going to be very difficult, isn't it? You must think me mad. If I start at the beginning, too many silly stories will cloud your understanding." His eyes twinkled. "Even my name will do that."

"Your name? Are you not Professor Ambrose?"

"Actually, yes, I am. My books are published in the name of Professor M. Ambrose. The M stands for Merlin."

The old gentleman watched the range of expressions play across Rhea's face, from bewilderment to disbelief, before settling on gradual wonder as part of the vision became clearer.

"Merlin Ambrosius. Magician to King Arthur. Apart from the time lapse it makes a strange kind of sense, I suppose." Rhea shook her head and laughed at herself, caught in the moment. "How old are you?"

"About 1500, I think, though," he added with a twinkle, "it is a little hard to be precise, you understand. I may be immortal, I'm not altogether sure. I aged as any man until Arthur's death, and then I seemed to stop. It has to do with the swords, you know." Rhea didn't and said so.

"I am the Keeper of Light for this age of the world. The swords are the weapons of the Champions. Arthur was a Champion for his age. Over the centuries, the nations of the world have become so intertwined that the task has grown. We who are now called are responsible for bringing our race into the new age which is dawning.

"In other times, others have been chosen to guard the hearts of men, yet at the end, if we prevail, all must meet in harmony. If we fail, then the cycle of destruction will begin again." The old man regarded her gravely. "Child, I believe you to be one of the Champions for this age of the world. Will you help me? It is a hard choice to make and I must ask you to consider it well before you answer."

Rhea felt her head was spinning with the incredible things she was being asked to believe, yet there was a sincerity in the old man's pain that rang true and a palpable tension in the air.

Then there was the Professor's inexplicable knowledge of her dream and the incident today.

For some reason she could not, in the cold light of logic, explain, Rhea felt that the bizarre tale was true.

"I told you once before, that I wouldn't run away, Professor... Merlin," she said. The old gentleman's eyes flickered at her use of his name. "But I would appreciate an answer to all of my questions. What happened last time?"

"Thank you for your trust, my child," he replied. Then he squared his shoulders as if to face an enemy. "The call came in 1788, the year before the revolution in France. I chose the wrong man for the task and my failure began the series of events which took Europe through the Crimean war, Communism and two World Wars. The stakes, you see, are desperately high and the burden is always carried by ordinary men and women like yourself."

The magnitude of the pain the old man carried shocked Rhea. She could not imagine the weight of the centuries of guilt which he bore. It explained why he was so determined now not to commit another such error.

She was being given every opportunity to decline and knew that she would not. If he was deluded, his delusion held more reality for her than anything she had felt before.

"What happens next?"

An expression of profound relief flitted across the face of legend, followed by his irrepressible chuckle.

"To be perfectly honest, I don't know!" Rhea gasped but Merlin held up a hand. "Now, don't panic, I know what needs to be done, I just don't know yet how or where. We have to find the first sword and the message you were given today holds the key. We shall also need help; this is not something we need to do alone. I have a feeling our company is almost complete. If I read the signs aright, both Alec and Jamie have their part in this."

"Do they know any of this?"

"Not yet. Alec took Jamie off for dinner with Elizabeth tonight, she will do him good. The lad was rather concerned about you. Had I not acquired my medical training many years ago, I fancy he would have called an ambulance instead of calling home. I hardly like to tell him," Merlin added mischievously, "that I first learned the art of healing from the local wise woman in my youth! They'll be back shortly," he added looking at a large silver pocket watch, "it's almost eleven and Elizabeth tends not to stay up later than that."

This piece of information surprised Rhea. She could not imagine any woman inviting Alec to dinner, after an interrupted lunch, only to have him leave at ten thirty. Her puzzled expression was not lost on her companion whose knowledge of human hearts had been gleaned over more than a millennium.

"You will like Elizabeth, Rhea. She is a wonderful woman, very beautiful still despite her age and ill health." He paused to watch this information sink in. "Sabrina looks very much like her, but Alec takes after his father."

"She's Alec's mother?"

"Why, yes child, he is entitled to one you know." Rhea realised her employer was making fun of her. She also realised that they both knew why and blushed.

Merlin lifted her chin and looked long into her eyes, his own very serious for once. "Do not run away from this either, daughter. You have wrought a great change in Alec already; he has been more alive today than I have seen him in a long while. I have no doubt that his mother has noticed the change this evening too and she has long been concerned about the fences he has erected around himself. Alec is a good man to have as a friend."

The crunch of car tyres on gravel signalled the end of the interview and Merlin left Rhea with the injunction to go back to bed. He made a show of gathering up the supper tray to take back to the house.

"Sleep well, child. And bless you. I shall talk with Alec and Jamie tonight and we'll see where tomorrow leads us."

Balancing the precarious pile of crockery the old man departed, leaving Rhea with much to consider.

She locked the door and took the tea tray out to the kitchen where she stood for a long time staring through the uncurtained window at the stars.

She was beginning to understand that her perception of the world in which she lived had just been turned upside down and she felt uncertain of her place in the new scheme of things. She knew nothing of swords or immortals and she certainly didn't feel like a Champion of Light. Strangely, the one thing she found easiest to accept was the Professor's avowed identity. There was neither rhyme nor reason to it, she simply believed him.

Rhea wondered what the men at the Lodge would make of it all and that turned her thoughts to Alec.

Alec Graham, bachelor at forty-three? Forty-four? Rhea didn't know. An invalid mother who lived apart from him somehow, but with whom he evidently spent much time; a younger sister who ran a bookshop for him; a failed engagement. Rhea had few other facts to consider.

She knew he could be kind and gentle and he could obviously be counted on to help a friend in need, though Rhea didn't flatter herself that he had come running on her behalf. It was for Jamie and the Professor he had responded so quickly. Rhea set little store by Merlin's teasing, she and Alec barely knew each other, had only met at breakfast for the first time… was it really only that morning? … and he had treated her with formal disapproval.

This afternoon's escapade could only be regarded as both embarrassing and troublesome and the kindness he had shown as a reflexive response to a fellow human being in distress. At best perhaps he would be a little less formal next time they met.

Rhea dried the cups and did as the Professor instructed. She went to bed.

Chapter Four

"HOLY ART THOU"

Alec watched from the door as the green robed figure before the easel wielded a paintbrush like a magic wand. Rhea was unaware of his presence as she tried to capture the vision of the stones. It had seemed important to try and preserve as much of the image as she could and she was working in oils, in a bold impressionistic style in an attempt to portray the light, movement and power of what she had witnessed.

Merlin had said that the vision could hold a clue and she was determined not to let time or sleep further blunt the clarity of her memory.

She stepped back to examine the painting, pushing a stray curl back from her face. There was a ruined castle by a river and a figure clothed in translucent rainbows holding a sword, hilt uppermost, in its hands, obscuring the features. Green fields stretched away into the distance while the horizon was dominated by the distinctive silhouette of a mountain.

Her concentration broken, Rhea became aware that she was not alone and turned, startled, to see who was there. Alec stepped forward into the pool of light.

"I'm sorry to disturb you, I've just left Ambrose and saw the glow though the skylight. I didn't expect you to be up, let alone out here at this time. It is after three, you know." His tone once more held disapproval, but Rhea knew that it was prompted by concern, rather than dislike.

"If you have been with the Professor until this time yourself, then he must have explained everything to you."

"As much as he could explain of such a fantastic tale, yes." The tone was noncommittal and there was only one way she was going to find out what Alec had made of it all.

"Did you believe him?"

"Oddly enough, yes I did, though I admit it took me a while. Jamie found it all rather easier to accept, I think. No doubt that young man is fast asleep, dreaming of swords and sorcery and damsels in distress." The oblique reference to their earlier encounter made Rhea turn away to hide her flushed cheeks.

"I'm sorry. I didn't want to upset you, Rhea." Alec took a breath. "I'm not very good at this, am I? My mother tells me my manners are appalling and I'm afraid she is right, as usual." Alec ran a hand through his hair in apparent frustration and the gesture made him look far less sure of himself than Rhea had hitherto believed.

"Alec," she began trying to choose the right words, "you gave me just what I needed this afternoon and I am grateful for your care." Rhea's tone laid a particular emphasis on the last word which conveyed far more than the words itself. "We got off to a poor start this morning, shall we try again?" She smiled and Alec took the hand she extended to him in friendship, raising it to his lips in a courtly manner.

"Thank you." Alec's own slow smile answered hers. "Now, perhaps you could satisfy my curiosity. Just what *are* you doing out here at this time of night?"

Rhea told him of the nagging sense of purpose which had kept her awake and forced her out to the studio. The two turned to inspect the painting and after studying it for a few minutes Alec asked what reference materials she had used, indicating the bookshelf with a wave of his hand.

"None. Why do you ask?"

"I think I recognise the place." Alec began to rifle through the miniature library, checking and discarding volume after volume in silence until he found what he sought. "Look at this. Recognise anything?"

The colour plate showed a ruin in a field. In the background was the unmistakable outline of the fell in Rhea's painting.

"Where is this?" she asked, reading the caption beneath the picture. "Mallerstang Edge. I've never heard of it. Is it far from here?"

"The hill in the distance is called Wild Boar Fell, not far from Kirkby Stephen, about fifty miles away. The ruins are the remains of Pendragon Castle, where legend says Uther Pendragon, King Arthur's father, was born. I think Ambrose has his clue."

The two shared a look of astonishment, events seemed to be conspiring to banish any lingering doubts they might have harboured as to their own, and the Professor's, sanity.

"I think we will be taking a trip there in the near future," said Alec. "This is ridiculous! Twenty four hours ago all this would have seemed like arrant nonsense to me." He grinned rather ruefully. "I suppose I'll even have to apologise to my little sister for making fun of all her New Age mumbo jumbo too. She will never let me live it down."

"My daughter, Anna, will be terribly disappointed to be missing all of this. She is working her way round Europe with friends at present."

"How old is she?"

"Twenty one. Your sister? Sabrina, isn't it?"

"Almost twenty." They exchanged a smile of mutual sympathy. "Well, at least that's one thing we have in common." Alec looked at his watch. "Good grief, look at the time and I promised Ambrose I'd be back for breakfast. I must go and you should really be in bed. Come on, lock up here and I'll walk you back to the cottage."

Rhea washed her brushes in turpentine, covered her palette and switched off the lights. She shivered a little in the night air and Alec quickly draped his coat around her shoulders, ignoring her protest. He waited until Rhea had turned on the light in the cottage before taking his leave of her. Rhea was unaware that he had also waited to hear the key turn in the lock before walking away.

By eight thirty next morning, Rhea and the three men had repaired to the Professor's study to allow Mrs Long to launch an assault on the breakfast table. Both Rhea and Alec looked tired, but Jamie was livelier than ever, a fact noted with indulgent amusement by the older members of the group.

Rhea had carefully transported the wet canvas to the Lodge before breakfast and set it on the sketching easel in the room, where it had been intently examined. Both Jamie and Merlin agree that a trip to the spot had become the next priority, to which end Jamie had been dispatched to wheedle Mrs Long into preparing a picnic for four.

The fifty mile trip along winding roads would take the best part of two hours, so an early start was desirable. Alec and Rhea, having anticipated the trip, were both dressed for walking, and they agreed to meet in fifteen minutes.

Rhea flew back to the cottage to grab hiking boots and a warm coat, calling at the studio to collect her field kit. She arrived at the Lodge to find the study empty and passed the time browsing the Professor's collection of rare, early books and artefacts. The dawning realisation that many of these ancient things could have been with their owner since they were first made struck her forcibly and left her awed at the dimly perceived centuries that Merlin had survived.

Most moving were the simple items; a bone flute, a small wooden horse which looked as if it had been carved for a child, a rough, earthenware bowl. So engrossed had she become that she didn't hear the Professor until he was standing at her side and she turned with a guilty start to meet the kindness in his eyes. She indicated the treasures on the shelves with a helpless gesture.

"All these years, so many people. How do you bear it?"

"Because I must, child. The gods made it so and I must follow the path they have shaped for me." The old man smiled gently as if to offer her comfort for the centuries of loss that she had dimly understood. He crossed to a glazed cabinet and unlocked it, selecting a small item and holding it out to Rhea. "Wear this for me, child. She who wore it first would be proud for you to wear it now and remember her."

The old man who was also Merlin, slipped a ring onto the third finger of her right hand where, by good luck or magic, it fitted perfectly. The broad band of reddish gold was skilfully carved with an intricate spiral design and set with a clear polished stone that caught and held the light.

Rhea could think of nothing adequate to say, so she leaned over and kissed the old man on the cheek.

"The stone, though uncut, is a diamond," he explained, "The Romans had been using them for years. The name diamond comes from the Greek 'adamas' which means 'invincible'. It is an appropriate gift for what we must attempt."

"Who wore it first, Professor?"

"A lady much maligned by the tales now told. They say she bound me in crystal but in truth, the only prison was her heart. She loved me as I loved her, but I was not free to live and love as other men. My task was to build a kingdom, not a hearth and I lost her. She waited for me all her life, but as she grew old, I aged not at all. She could not have understood, although she herself was a priestess of the Mother. The ring was her gift to me."

"Nimue?"

"Yes, child, that was her name," ageless grief in his voice. "Wear her ring and let her love be remembered."

The ensuing silence was broken by Jamie, suitably, if gaudily, attired and clutching an assortment of maps. He was followed seconds later by Alec and the three younger members turned expectantly towards the Professor whose habitual expression of amusement had been replaced by one of grim determination.

"You are all now aware of the nature of the task we are about to undertake. Once begun, there can be no turning back. I ask you all to search within your heart of hearts before we go any further. I cannot tell you what you will be called upon to endure, because I do not know. All I can say is that the danger must not be underestimated; we shall not be allowed to go unopposed. I am not without power, but I cannot guarantee the safety of any one of you." The old man subjected each one to a searching stare. "Jamie, you are the youngest of us all and I love you like a son. This is not some high romantic tale of knights in armour. Will you commit yourself to the fight?"

Jamie met his mentor's eyes with love and answered without hesitation.

"I will."

"Alec, you, I think, will be the leader in much of this. Succeed or fail, can you carry the burden, are you strong enough to admit your own weaknesses and let others lead where you cannot?" The old man locked his gaze with Alec and the watchers were aware of a wordless communication between them.

"I do not know, but I will try. I will go where you guide us." Merlin nodded as if satisfied and turned finally to Rhea.

"Child, you have already suffered in this battle and understand more, perhaps, than your companions the nature of the forces with which we will be working. You could not be blamed if you turned to follow your own road now. You have served the Light all your life without knowing its name. Will you choose now to serve with us and take up the gauntlet as a Champion of Light?" The old man's eyes were kind as he awaited her reply.

"You said once that you were right to choose me. I don't know if that's true, but I have made my choice and will follow you."

Merlin smiled his approval.

"My dear, you may lead us all yet."

The old man turned away from them a moment and could be observed to make use of a large white handkerchief. He cleared his throat and spoke again,

"Thank you, thank you all. Now, before we leave there is something I feel we should do. You have given yourselves into the service of the Light. No matter by what name each of us calls our god or gods, the Light which inspires our faith is the same. Let us ask the blessing of the One upon our company." He held out his hands for Jamie and Rhea and motioned for Alec to do likewise.

"Close your eyes if it helps and imagine that we are bound together by a cord of shining blue. See it clearly in your mind; make it real in your imagination until you can feel the touch of the cord on your skin. Now, imagine that a dome of clear white light is spreading out around us and encompassing us, swirling like mist, but holding its shape. The light protects and guards us." The old man spoke clearly and calmly, his voice exercising a hypnotic effect on the other three, who could see and feel the scene unfold as he described it.

"The dome begins to spin, clockwise, until the shape distorts and becomes a funnel reaching up into infinity. Let each send their soul free through the vortex and make the unreserved dedication to the Light."

Silence held the room as several minutes ticked by unnoticed. A voice resonant with power broke the stillness in ancient prayer,

"Holy art Thou, Lord of the Universe,

Holy art Thou, whom Nature hath not formed,

Holy art Thou, the vast and the mighty One,

Lord of the Light and of the Darkness."

Rhea, Jamie and Alec were aware that this was the Merlin of old who spoke. The voice of power and prophecy that had earned him his place in the legends of the world.

"I bring into Thy Light these three to be Thy Champions. Wilt Thou accept their service, freely given and grant them Thy blessing?"

The room brightened and began to glow and waver until it became a dazzling golden hall. Tall pillars limned with iridescent flame seemed to stretch to infinity in all directions and a fragrance like all the flowers of Eden filled the air.

They turned as one towards the Presence that all sensed was there. None could see the form of that Great One; all were suffused with joy and humility that they had been granted this gift. They bowed in awe as they felt a great Hand laid over them in blessing and acceptance and each felt the bereavement when Merlin finally spoke again,

"It is done." The glow receded and the room took on its accustomed aspect. "See now the dome thin and waver, dissipating like smoke in the breeze. Watch as the cords thin to nothingness. You are returned."

Merlin watched as the three returned to themselves, noting the inner radiance that shone from three pairs of eyes, reluctant to release the lambent splendour of the vision they had shared. He held up his hand to still the spate of questions which were inevitable.

"There are some things which are better not discussed. Accept what you have been granted. You may call it magic," he glanced at Jamie, "or simple hypnosis if you will," a look at Alec, "what you think, does not really matter. What you have witnessed may only be judged in your hearts and by the effect it has on your lives. The means do not matter."

Rhea felt she would never again be the same. Now she knew what they were fighting for and understood that for her, no sacrifice would be too great to defend the Light she had been shown.

Chapter Five

PENDRAGON CASTLE

The drive to Mallerstang took a little less than two hours, passing through the spectacular limestone landscape of the Dales. Rhea was enchanted by the moors and crags and fascinated by the ageless meanderings of the dry stone walls between which the road twisted and turned. The journey was enlivened by Jamie's re-telling of some of the legends associated with the sites they passed, aided occasionally by Merlin. Rhea was learning to accept his identity, but still found it difficult at times, as when the old man corrected Jamie on some point of legend by giving the remembered account of its origins.

They parked the car as close as possible to the ruins of Pendragon Castle, with Alec and Jamie shouldering the bulging backpacks containing Mrs Long's idea of a light lunch. Merlin set off at a brisk pace and the others followed him along the road and over a stile. There in a corner of the field stood the birthplace of Uther. The castle seemed forlorn and forgotten in the sunlight, the arch of the doorway standing open to the sheep and the winds and the few remaining windows framing only the sky.

"It was a good place to build," said Merlin, staring at the castle and seeing far more than his companions.

In the sunlight below them sparkled the waters of the Eden. The castle itself stood on a small hillock and was framed by the valley sides; to the right the towering cliffs of Mallerstang Edge, to the left, the Nab of Wild Boar Fell.

"There were trees here once, long ago, as I recall." The old man focused his gaze back on the present and his tone became matter of fact. "Mind, the original castle was much older than this one. I suppose the place has been inhabited since long before my time. The stories say Uther was born here, but to be honest, I can't say if that is true. Uther and I never had much time for each other and didn't waste words in idle chat. Apart from a few state occasions my presence was not required at Uther's court once he succeeded his brother. Only once did he ask for my help and that story is still well known."

Alec and Rhea exchanged incredulous glances. Jamie was almost beside himself with excitement as Merlin told the age-old story they had all dismissed as legend... until now.

"Uther wanted Ygraine of Tintagel, but she was already wife to one of his most loyal chieftains. Do you know Tintagel Castle? It stands on a spit of land that is almost an island and could only be reached by a wooden bridge. You can imagine how easy it was for Gorlois to guard his wife there. A mere handful of men could prevent anyone entering that castle."

The old man chuckled, his eyes seemed far away and long ago.

"They still call it a rape, but Ygraine was a young woman, proud and passionate and Gorlois an old man. It was no rape.

"With Ygraine's help and a scanty disguise it took only a small illusion created from the mists to bemuse the guards and the thing was done. Not even for Britain would I have assisted at a rape."

A cloud crossed Merlin's features.

"Her lord died that night in a rash attack on Uther's camp. That I had not foreseen. Uther wed Ygraine before Gorlois was cold in his grave and nine months later Arthur was born. My part in the affair inevitably leaked out and I was called the king's whoremaster and worse. Arthur had to be fostered given that the timing of his birth raised questions of his legitimacy. I took him away to safety where he could grow in peace. The rest, as they say, is history. Or legend." The old man shrugged his shoulders and turned, chuckling at the spellbound expressions of his audience. "It's an old story."

"Yes," gasped Jamie," but it's the first time we've heard it told first hand!"

"You'll get used to it, you know," said Merlin in sympathy. Jamie muttered something inaudible and walked off to inspect the ruins. The others followed, with Alec asking what the next move was likely to be. "No idea, lad, none at all. We simply follow our hunches at this stage. Any ideas?"

"Where did you find Excalibur, the first time?" asked Rhea.

"It was given into my care by the Lady of Avalon. She was High Priestess of the Mother on the Isle of Apples, close to where Glastonbury stands today. We will not find the answer in the past, child, though the past may well point the way."

The three followed Jamie through the low arch of the empty doorway and into the enclosure formed by the crumbling walls. They found Jamie on his knees before a shimmering figure robed in rainbows like moonlight on water. Jamie's face was radiant, his expression rapt as he gazed at the apparition. Merlin moved to stand behind the boy while Rhea and Alec took up positions either side of the kneeling youth.

"Welcome, ancient one. It is long since we met." The voice was deep and rich and seemed to come from a great distance. "You have chosen well in this one, but your company is not yet complete, the Bearer of Flame is not yet among you."

The figure turned a searching gaze on Rhea and Alec in turn.

"Be welcome here, Heart of Earth, yours shall be the first task and the first trial. Be welcome also Master of Air, learn that Love is mightier than reason"

The spectral gaze now rested once again on Jamie. "Water-bearer, you are the Herald of the Age which dawns. Courage will be needed. Ancient One, as always you are the Keeper and the catalyst. You have long borne the grief of failure, shouldering the blame for centuries of pain and suffering. Do you still not understand that only through the birth pangs of conflict could mankind learn and grow? You did not fail. It was not time.

"Ah Merlin, forgive yourself at last, my son." The last phrase sounded almost human in its grief and Merlin, old beyond belief, wept like a child. The figure held up his hand to forestall a question. "No, my son, you could not have been given this comfort earlier, time runs its own speed in the Otherworld as well you know and you, also, had to grow and learn. Grief has taught you much and you have grown in wisdom since last we met. Have not all the Light-Bearers suffered?"

The hand was now extended in benediction over the company.

"Daughter, yours is to be the first trial. You must defeat fear in the place of the Stone Giants. Do not falter." Rhea could make no sense of this and looked to Merlin for guidance. There came the familiar rich chuckle, but not from its usual source. "My son, would you like a guide?"

"Father, no. You wouldn't!" cried Merlin, a note of desperation in his voice.

"But yes, my son. Your brother is doing nothing of any great import just now. He will help you on your way. It is my wish."

There was a distinct suggestion of laughter in the air as the vision faded from sight, leaving in its wake the fragrance of new grass and woodland flowers. Merlin stood, head in hands, mumbling to himself. The others did not know what to do as he was obviously upset.

"You don't understand what he has done and he is enjoying it!" said Merlin quite suddenly. "Whose side is he on? He said you would be put to the test first, Rhea. But no, he has to inflict this on me instead!" The old gentleman stomped off leaving his companions wide eyed in astonishment.

"We've just met one of the Old Gods, unless I'm mistaken; the second Divinity we've encountered today. And Merlin is annoyed with him?" The incongruity of this struck the three of them and tension dissolved into laughter. "More than anything else I've seen this convinces me he really is the Merlin of old. No-one else could react like that."

Alec and Rhea were inclined to agree. Difficult as it was to assimilate the strange experiences of the day, it seemed incomprehensible that anyone could treat the apparition to a show of irritation without being on very familiar terms with it.

"Merlin called him Father. I wonder…"

"You're right," replied Rhea. "I think perhaps we should go and find him, don't you?" She set off after Merlin.

They found him seated on a boulder in the sunshine where they had left the backpacks earlier. He looked round ruefully at their approach and began to unpack lunch.

"We may as well eat while you give me the third degree," he sighed. "I imagine you have plenty of questions. Pass the coffee, Jamie. Rhea, ladies first." Rhea's question was possibly the easiest to ask, though probably one of the hardest to answer.

"Your father? Or was that a form of address?"

"Both really," Merlin replied, selecting a sandwich from the box beside him. "He is Cernunnos, the Horned One, the Forest Lord, god of the wild creatures, guardian of cosmic truth, giver of prosperity and good fortune," Merlin looked innocently round the circle while Jamie choked, "And fertility, of course. He likes that part best. Which is why I come from such a large and varied family."

Merlin ate the sandwich as he watched his listeners begin to digest the information. As the implications of his bald statement began to register on their faces, he continued.

"My mother was the daughter of a Welsh chieftain. She was in the beech woods, collecting berries and saw a beautiful white stag. Not very original. Predictably, she followed it and became separated from the rest of the party... you can guess the rest, I imagine."

Rhea blushed and Jamie's eyes took on the familiar sparkle. Alec merely raised his eyebrows and waited.

"The following summer I was born, causing more than the usual amount of gossip. For while the village maids could breed where they would, the Chieftain's daughter was supposed to be a little more circumspect. The true story got out and spread. It was far less unusual than you would think today, except for the lady's status. So it was readily believed.

"I grew up an outsider, even the adults made the sign against the evil eye as I passed and the other children, only half understanding, shunned me. I took to straying from the village and out onto the hills or into the woods. The animals learned to trust me and became my friends and playmates. It took me a long time to realise that it was not usual for them to talk to humans or that I could understand them and it wasn't until I came across my father that I realised I was related to many of them. Being a god does allow for a certain freedom in the choice of shape one can assume."

Jamie was silently shaking with laughter by this time and Merlin glared at him fiercely, the humour creeping back into his own voice in response to the young man's mirth.

"You may laugh all you like, but think of the complications of having a rabbit for a sibling!" Jamie howled and collapsed in a helpless heap on the grass. His laughter was infectious and both Alec and Rhea were struggling. "I'm probably related to half the rabbits in Britain by now."

Realising that there was little point in continuing the narrative until the three had laughed themselves back to normality, Merlin helped himself to one of Jamie's scones. He was on his second by the time the trio had settled enough to ask him to continue.

"I learned much from my extended family about the ways of nature and from my father I learned to control the gifts that my parentage had given me. I had the talent for prophecy and for conversing with creatures of the Otherworld. Shape changing was more difficult to master, but my half brothers and sisters were patient teachers and I enjoyed it all." Jamie choked but received a quelling stare from the old man. "No, before you ask, I left that to my sire."

"You could tell them about that pretty young doe."

"That is none of their… oh god."

"Not quite, but close, dear brother! Well met, Merlin!" The dismay on the old man's face was too much for Jamie, who went off into fresh peals of laughter.

Rhea blinked in astonishment as a small figure seemed to step out of the air before her. He looked to be about twelve years old, but Rhea was fast learning not to make any logical assumptions. Untidy chestnut curls framed a face brimming with glee, his only garment was a strip of animal skin around his hips and about his brow was a garland of oak leaves and bright berries. Despite his apparent youth there was a disturbing and cynical quality to his face. Rhea thought it lacked humanity. He reminded her of the classical Greek portrayal of a satyr.

"No, my lady, a satyr is not what I am." Rhea had not spoken aloud and her silent consternation elicited a gleeful response from the newcomer.

"But satire is one of his vices," interposed a disgruntled Merlin.

"Bravo, brother mine! Perhaps there is hope for you yet."

"Not while you are around!" The creature greeted this sally with light laughter and Rhea decided that this battle of word and wit had probably been going on for centuries. No offence seemed to be taken despite the content of the exchange. It occurred to Rhea that this was the verbal sparring of two who were not only familiar, but fond of each other too. The youth smiled wickedly at Rhea and leaned close,

"Don't tell Merlin. He'd be terribly upset if he thought I knew that. You are most perceptive, my lady." He sketched a mocking blow in her direction then seated himself cross legged on the grass. "Are you not going to introduce me to your flock, brother?" Merlin glared at him.

"You will doubtless have informed yourself of their identities already," said the old man.

"My gifts have their uses, I admit," shrugged the youth.

"It is unusual to hear you admit to anything," was the riposte. "Rhea, Jamie, Alec… I am afraid I must introduce my half-brother, Heilyn. You could try and guard your thoughts but it is probably quite useless to do so as he has little respect for etiquette and has probably gleaned as much as he wishes to know already." Heilyn assumed an air of innocence completely at odds with the brilliant eyes. For some unaccountable reason Rhea found herself blushing. "You will have guessed that we share a father, but Heilyn's mother is not human."

"Is not?" asked Alec. Heilyn inclined his head in an uncharacteristic gesture of respect.

"My mother rules in Faery as ever. Time touches the Otherworld differently. I am actually some years older than Merlin." Merlin muttered something unintelligible under his breath.

"How much older?" This from Jamie.

"A couple of thousands of your years or so, give or take the odd century or two." Jamie's jaw dropped in surprise. "Consider… my father is a god, my mother immortal, my own nature determines my appearance unless I will a change. How should I look any different?"

"Heilyn," said Rhea, beginning to comprehend, "*what* are you?"

"I am of the realm of Faery and of the Earth; I am the spirit of spring in the oak, the song of the brook and the flight of the lark. I am the dew on the primrose and the star in the dark. And for this time, lady, I am the servant of the Champions of Light."

"Will you guide us?"

"It is permitted. However, I may not intervene directly." Merlin shot a suspicious look as his sibling. "Your task is of this world and I am of another. Only where the worlds meet have I a place in your quest."

Alec had been listening closely to this exchange,

"Your father, Cernunnos, told us that the first trial would be for Rhea. Are we permitted to help her?"

"You must. Rhea must go to the place of the Stone Giants. You know it as Trollers Gill. There is an old danger there that has been reawakened."

Silence fell over the company, each occupied with their own thoughts and fears. Jamie was first to speak again,

"Are we allowed any more clues to this puzzle, Heilyn?"

"You do not need them, you already know the answers. You just need to know the questions."

"Why must you speak in riddles?" demanded Merlin. "It was always one of your more annoying habits!"

Heilyn simply laughed in reply, then added,

"Two reasons. The first is to make you think for yourselves. You, my brother, know the value of such teaching. Your friends cannot rely on luck or divine intervention to help them succeed."

Merlin sighed and agreed reluctantly.

"And the second reason?"

Heilyn began to fade until there remained only a silver shimmer in the air accompanied by a gay chuckle,

"Because it annoys you, brother dear!" said the empty air.

On the way home, Merlin was pressed to explain his relationship to

Heilyn and Cernunnos.

"… I wouldn't care to say who was the seducer and who the seduced in that alliance. Heilyn's mother is, of course, as beautiful as she chooses to be. Or perhaps it is more accurate to say that she is as lovely as the desire of her hapless victims can perceive her."

"'Hapless'? Your father?" asked Jamie blandly, earning himself another quelling stare from Merlin.

"I have no doubt my father was more than willing," replied the mage. "Though whether it was desire or politics that brought them together I do not know. Any offspring of such a union is a joint decision, usually with some specific purpose in mind. I have yet to determine whether my father's only purpose in allowing the creation of Heilyn was to have him ready to plague me as soon as I understood the nature of my heritage."

The gruff tone made Rhea smile, while the irrepressible Jamie bit his lip. Alec, who was driving them home, encouraged Merlin to elaborate.

"A faery birth is nothing like its human equivalent."

Jamie nodded sagely, in imitation of his older friend,

"Cabbage patches and gooseberry bushes," was his cryptic remark.

"Actually, you're not too far wrong. The child is created from the essence of the beings as they mate, drawing on the elements of Nature to be ensouled, so to speak, in the new life. When Heilyn answered Rhea's question he was not just being irritatingly poetic. In a very real sense he is the spirit of the oak and dew on the flowers."

Merlin paused for the next question, but his companions were silent.

"I realise how difficult all this is, but you must get used to dealing with strange concepts fairly rapidly. Events are moving quicker that I had expected and we seem to be getting rather a lot of help. It doesn't normally happen this way and it makes me wonder how much stronger the Enemy has become since our last encounter."

"Merlin," asked Rhea, "what is the Otherworld?"

"That's a hard one to answer. There are many realms in the Otherworld. Some, like Heilyn's home, border this world closely and its creatures can be seen readily by the inhabitants of our own. Others are so far removed from our experience that they are almost impossible to grasp. The creatures of Faery have given us many myths and we may feel a kind of familiarity when we meet them. But myth is not truth.

"Heilyn's mother, for instance, is no Titania. By human standards she can be cruel and heartless and her morals non-existent. You may not judge by the accepted code of our world. Faery is not immoral, but amoral in our terms. A leopard is beautiful and dangerous; it kills and devours its prey with dreadful ferocity and mates where it will. It is not evil, it follows the dictates of its own nature and instinct, yet in a human such behaviour would be condemned. So it is with the Otherworld. An ogre will rip you to shreds but it is not personal. Just a method of food preparation."

Merlin gave them a few moments to digest this comment, their revulsion causing the glimmer of a smile.

"The next question is where are these other worlds, to which the answer is 'right here'," he continued. "They permeate our world in the same way as radio waves fill the air. Imagine the thousands of different broadcasts being transmitted at any time. They are all around us, unseen and unheard. They can only be deciphered with the right equipment and then they may only be clearly heard if that equipment is correctly tuned. And," he paused to emphasise the next point, "can only be understood if you choose to listen.

"There are places where the worlds touch, their frequencies compatible. The veil is thin at the ancient sites. Most people are sensitive to their atmosphere to some degree. You three are all attuned to the life in the land and can feel more than many. You do, of course, have help and those on the other side are meeting you halfway. The battle for the Light transcends the veil and the choices made by creatures of all the worlds are essentially the same, in spite of their disparate natures. Understand this. The choices you make will echo through all the worlds."

"Then, if these worlds are real and legend has a basis in fact," mused Alec, "then the gods, all the gods, are real too? We met the Horned One today and something else this morning which seemed divine to me." The others nodded in agreement.

"The gods," replied Merlin, "are both real and mere figments of our collective imagination." The old man chuckled at the consternation on Jamie's face. "Yes, it is the great paradox.

"Man saw many marvels in the world when it was young. They saw that light meant life, so they worshipped the sun. By their worship the star became a deity in their eyes, but they had no abstract concept of godhead and imagined a sun god in humanised form to which they could relate. Their faith and worship were so strong, the vision of their god so concrete in their mind, that their collective prayer built a thought form on the Inner Planes. Because the principle behind their worship was a reality, the essence of that cosmic principle gave life to their god.

You could say that the gods as men have known them were created by man, but it would only be half a truth as the powers they represent existed before man walked the Earth. All the gods ever worshipped exist somewhere on the Inner Planes, waiting for their followers to call them back.

"However, most gods have many faces. The sun, the source of light and life has been worshipped by almost every community of mankind. Each aspect could be called by its particular devotees, but the power from whence the god took its being remained constant. At the end, there is but One, with countless faces. All the gods are one God; all the goddesses are one Goddess, all merely facets of a single jewel."

"What about Heilyn," asked Jamie, "where does he fit into all this?"

"Heilyn is, in our terms at least, far older than I. He was among my first playmates and was my first real teacher. He, like myself, is of two worlds and has access to many others; his knowledge is far wider than his appearance would indicate and as a guide his aid will be invaluable. Like his mother his morals leave much to be desired in this world, but like our father, he can be trusted implicitly in our quest. He is not merely a servant of the Light, but an aspect of Light personified.

"Unfortunately, he is also infuriating, unpredictable, irritating and erratic. He can, and will, read your thoughts and there is nothing you can do about it. While it may prove useful in helping you face your fears and uncertainties, he is unscrupulous enough to use what he finds for his own ends or entertainment.

"There are unspoken rules about intruding in the minds of your fellow creatures. Yes, I too can pick up on your thoughts, but will not do so without very good reason. You have all suspected this at some time, but I will not intrude without cause. I have lived in this world long enough to be able to read almost as much in the tone of a voice or turn of phrase and I can hear much in a silence."

Silence indeed followed this last avowal as each of the three younger members of the party struggled to come to terms with the new vision of the world they had been shown.

Alien though the concepts seemed at first, they all found it made a strange kind of sense and gradually, in the light of the day's experiences began to accept. Jamie was filled with a joyful wonder that the tales which had fascinated him all his life had taken on a life of their own. He felt as if he had stepped into a fairy tale and felt no fear, only excitement.

Rhea was afraid. She had no idea what she was expected to do. She did not see herself as courageous or exceptional in any way, yet her very acceptance of the task ahead showed her mettle. She had been used to seeing herself as a middle-aged widow whose only talent was painting. She would have been astonished had she known how much respect her strength and honesty had already earned her. She was only afraid that she would somehow fail her new friends.

Alec was worried too, but for Rhea's safety. He found himself increasingly aware of her and had watched her closely today, adding another dimension to his growing admiration. He would have liked to be able to talk to her again as they had last night; he felt there was a lot more to know about Rhea than most people would see. He wondered what his mother would make of her. Elizabeth missed very little that mattered.

Merlin had fears of his own. He alone knew the nature of their enemy and the kind of horrors they could be called upon to face. He was afraid to tell them too much lest their fear defeat them before they had begun, yet he knew they would have to be prepared. He hated having to send them into battle and would have chosen to carry the burden alone. His heart ached for them, yet he knew that having made their choice and been accepted, there was no way he could take the burden from them. These were the Champions of Light and they had made their dedication.

He was worried too by the absence of the last of their company as his father had mentioned. He could not see who this was to be. And this lack of knowledge was preying on his mind. He sent out a silent prayer for guidance and asked the Great Ones to watch over his fledgling army.

Chapter Six

ELIZABETH

Alec parked the car in front of a low cottage, waking Jamie who had been snoring for the last ten miles. The garden was an enchanting jumble of herbs and old roses, carefully planted to give the impression of chaos. The fragrance of thyme followed them as they walked to the green painted door. Alec lifted the latch and walked in, the others following. An elderly female in a fluffy cardigan appeared from the end of the passage in response to a greeting from Alec.

"Good afternoon, Gwen. Is my mother up to a little company for tea?"

"She is in the sunroom, Alec." The woman was short and quite slim, with bleached blonde hair curling incongruously about a face powdered and painted in a fashion forty years old. "Shall I tell her you are here or do you want to go through? Yes, go on through and I'll put the kettle on. Oh, Professor Ambrose, Elizabeth will be so pleased to see you!"

Eyelashes fluttered at the old gentleman in a manner which could only be described as coy. Merlin, to Rhea's delight, blushed and muttered something incoherent. Jamie came forward and gave Gwen a peck on the cheek and asked plaintively if she had no word of welcome for him.

"Oh, silly boy, we're always happy to see you. Are you hungry? Of course you are. I'll make some sandwiches too." The small figure flitted down the corridor in a flurry of pink skirts.

The sunroom was a bright apartment, painted in shades of golden yellow to enhance the light streaming through the windows which made up most of one long wall. A Chopin waltz was playing quietly in the background and an elderly Labrador slept in a patch of light, opening one eye to identify the visitors, before drifting back to sleep. Elizabeth was seated with her back to the window but rose as they entered.

"Alec, what a nice surprise! I didn't expect to see you until tomorrow." Alec caught her round the waist and placed a kiss on her cheek. "Jamie and Ambrose too, how lovely! You will stay for tea?"

"How are you Elizabeth? You look as beautiful as ever," said Merlin, taking his turn to embrace the lady. She was indeed very beautiful, despite her age, thought Rhea, who correctly guessed her to be around seventy. Almost as tall as her son, with silvery hair and a wonderful skin, as flawless and fragile as porcelain. She was dressed with casual elegance in a long amber gown with polished amber in her ears and in a great silver ring.

"Who is this, Ambrose? I can't tell," she asked, nodding towards Rhea.

"Such impatience! I would have introduced you in a second," Merlin chuckled and beckoned to Rhea to step closer. "This is Mrs Marchant. Rhea, I'd like you to meet my dear friend Elizabeth Graham, I know you have been curious about each other," he added with a mischievous grin. "Rhea has done some wonderful sketches of Pendragon Castle today. If the light is good enough for you perhaps she would like to show them to you."

"They are in the car, I'm afraid. I'll get them presently if you like," said Rhea, taking the outstretched hand.

"I would love to see them, but Jamie must run and fetch them now or else it will be too late." Rhea found this statement rather puzzling, but Elizabeth smiled and explained, "The menfolk have obviously forgotten to mention that I have a problem with my eyesight. I can see quite well in bright light, but am almost blind when the light fades. I became night-blind following a virus I picked up in Africa some years ago." She dismissed Rhea's surprise with a kindly squeeze of her hand, which she had not let go. "It serves me quite well, I assure you. Alec spoils me wonderfully and Gwennie mothers me. And having no real reason to stay up late I get plenty of beauty sleep," she quipped. "Come and sit with me, Rhea. I have heard so much about you since Ambrose found you."

Elizabeth led Rhea to a sofa next to the long window, while Alec and Merlin took chairs facing them. Jamie had scooted out to bring Rhea's sketch book.

"My eyes may not be much use but the rest of my senses are fine. What are you all up to?" The question had been addressed to Alec, who looked helplessly at Merlin. Elizabeth noted the exchanged and raised an eyebrow. "Ambrose?"

"It is time, Elizabeth dear, and these are the ones," he replied gravely. Elizabeth closed her eyes a moment and asked,

"Do they know?"

"Yes, I told them and they have already been accepted and received a blessing from Cernunnos, though it seems our company is incomplete."

Alec had been following this exchange with growing amazement. Having done some rapid calculations and decided that in this case two and two did make four, the shock which had held him dumb for several seconds finally released its strangle-hold on his tongue, allowing him the luxury of a single exclamation.

"Mother!" The word was both a question and an accusation, the reply little short of patronising, though there was laughter in the tone.

"Well, yes, dear. Of course. I've known for a long time. Merlin and I have been friends for over twenty years and I've known his identity for the last decade. Merlin is not an uncommon name in Wales, so I probably wouldn't have guessed if I hadn't overheard a long conversation between our friend and a grouse on the moor. Even that I would have put down to eccentricity or even … forgive me Merlin… senility, but a chance encounter with Merlin's brother left me in little doubt. Anyone whose brother can disappear at will into thin air has to be worth nagging for the truth."

"Your mother, you may have noticed," said Merlin with mock acidity, "nags very well."

"She also appears to be very good at keeping secrets. I had no inkling of any of this before you told us," replied Alec.

Jamie came back with the sketches and was rapidly brought up to date. Conversation became general as Gwen came in pushing a laden tea trolley. The birdlike lady fluttered and fussed over Elizabeth in a motherly way and flirted shyly with Merlin, who, for once, seemed at a loss. Elizabeth took Rhea to a desk with a bank of concealed spotlights to illuminate the paintings.

"These are quite lovely, Rhea You have a real feel for the country here." She lingered over a sketch that Rhea had made of the castle with Alec sprawled on a grassy bank below. Despite the strange happenings of the day, Rhea had thought he looked more at ease than she had seen him so far and had drawn him without his knowledge. "You have captured my son well. May I have this when you have done with it? It is rare to see Alec so relaxed. You appear to have made quite an impression on him in the last couple of days. Tell me, do you like him?"

"Really, I hardly know him yet."

"Now, don't be polite. My son is arrogant and bad mannered where women are concerned and yet you seem to have seen beyond that in this picture. Do you like him?"

"To be honest, I didn't at first. He was icily polite when we first met and Merlin's explanation just made me annoyed that he would tar all artists with the same brush." Elizabeth smiled, but nodded her understanding and encouraged her to continue. "I wasn't prepared to like him after that, I'm afraid. Then he was so kind and gentle when I was ill that he seemed like a different man. We talked for a while and things sort of straightened themselves out after that. I trust him and I'm glad he'll be with us in this. Yes, I do like him." Rhea was a little surprised to find that this was true.

"I'm glad. I think he will be too. He is neither as hard nor as invulnerable as he would like to believe and it's high time he was made to see that for himself." Rhea was surprised at the wry approval in the older woman's voice. Elizabeth turned the page. "Ah, I see you have met Heilyn too. Merlin must have been so pleased to see him!" Their friendship was cemented by a smile shared in affectionate amusement at Merlin's expense. The old gentleman, discretely monitoring the conversation, was well pleased with their reaction to each other.

Elizabeth resumed her seat near the window and allowed Gwen to pour her another cup of tea. Gwen was curious and asked Rhea all manner of questions. She begged for a peek at the paintings and was full of admiration. She shed a sympathetic tear when she learned Rhea was a widow and exclaimed at Anna's beauty when Rhea showed her the photo of her daughter that she carried in her handbag.

"You look far too young to have a daughter that age, Mrs Marchant. She's beautiful too. She doesn't look like you at all, does she? She must take after her poor father I suppose. Don't you think so Elizabeth?" She handed the photo to her friend who peered at it closely.

"She is certainly lovely, but I think she has something from her mother too." She held the picture for a moment before passing it wordlessly to Merlin, who studied the picture and nodded, as if to answer her question.

"May I?" asked Alec, "There is a resemblance, something about the eyes, I think."

Jamie was looking over Alec's shoulder with rapt attention.

"She looks like a mediaeval Madonna," was his only comment. Rhea, who knew her daughter well, laughed out loud. Anna was no saintly miss, but a very modern young woman with a mind of her own.

She could understand Jamie's comment though. Anna had grown into a beauty at some point in her teens. She had inherited Mike's colouring; her hair was long and she wore it parted in the centre so that it framed her face in silk like an Indian princess. It was a dramatic face, Rhea agreed, but it was hard to imagine anything less virginal than the denim shorts and cropped top that Anna wore in the photo.

To satisfy Gwen's curiosity, Rhea told her that Anna was touring Europe with friends, taking temporary jobs and making music to pay their way. Gwen seemed shocked that Rhea would allow her only daughter to go "traipsing round foreign parts" without being frantic with worry. Rhea laughed again.

"Anna is far wiser than I ever was at that age and she can take care of herself very well. Her friends are both sensible. Although they will have fun and probably do a few things I'd rather not know about, I know they will look after each other."

Gwen seemed ruffled by this attitude, so Elizabeth suggested that Alec show Rhea the garden, while Jamie helped her clear away the tea things,

"… which leaves Ambrose and I to chat for a while."

Alec complied readily enough, taking Rhea's elbow to guide her through the house to the back door. Laughter followed them as Jamie began the clearing up process by eating the last of the cake.

The walled garden behind the house was even more colourful than the front, with wide herbaceous borders and island beds defining graceful curves, leading the eye to new delights at every turn. Rhea was particularly impressed by a series of clay sculptures dotted here and there among the plants. The forms were softly flowing and full of movement, yet they looked almost unfinished. They reminded her of Rodin.

"Mmm, yes, Mother always admired his work and I've no doubt it influenced her own."

"Elizabeth made these? They are wonderful. No-one told me."

"She works through touch and often closes her eyes to feel what she is making. She only began to work in clay after her sight was damaged, as a kind of therapy and she has amazed us all. My mother is an incredible woman."

There was great love and respect in his voice and Rhea was again struck by the contradictions between his public and private faces. She felt privileged to be allowed to see him unmasked on such short acquaintance and guessed this was a rare thing.

"I can see she is very special. Everyone's tone changes when they speak of her, and having met her I can begin to understand why. Merlin told me she was a remarkable woman. That seems an understatement. Jamie adores her, that is obvious, and so does Gwen."

"Gwen was my father's secretary and was heartbroken when he died. Mother asked her to come and work for her here and it has been a great success for both of them. Gwen feels she is needed and has someone to love, while Mother is cared for twenty four hours a day by someone who is utterly devoted to her. It is a strange ménage as they have little in common, but they get along well together and I know I need never worry about Mother while Gwen is there to guard her." Again Alec had surprised her. Rhea did not think he was one to suffer fools gladly, yet he obviously valued the little woman for all the right reasons and was patently fond of her.

They strolled down the path bathed in early evening sunshine, stopping to admire Elizabeth's work amid the flowers. Beneath an old hawthorn tree they found a small statue almost flowing from the earth beside a small pool. The two stood in silence contemplating the figure. Rhea broke the silence this time,

"She said she had met Heilyn; it seems she understood him better than we did." The clay figure seemed to belong where it had been placed, in some indefinable fashion. The rough surfaces gave the impression of antiquity and the half formed features were clearly those of the mocking immortal. Rhea wondered how often the two had met and she marvelled at the life so captured in clay.

"My mother seems to have understood a good deal," Alec commented with a wry smile. "I find it hard to grasp that she should have known about Merlin and all the other strange folk for so long and never let anything slip. I doubt if I could have kept such a momentous secret for a decade. We are lucky, being part of a group at least we can share our experiences. We have each other."

"Yes, we have each other," she echoed, the knowledge a comforting spar in these strange waters.

Alec took her arm and led Rhea to a seat among the roses. Rhea sat, while Alec turned his back and stared out over a sea of flowers. She wondered what he was thinking, but dare not ask, so she waited, hoping the man would tell her what was on his mind. The sunlight on the back of his head showed the lighter strands of grey and gold in his hair. His back was a straight as his mother's, the shoulders broad and square. Rhea thought the stance epitomised the man but made any attempt at intimacy all the harder. The broad shoulders relaxed a little and he sighed, turning back to Rhea,

"Are you afraid of what we're getting into?"

"Yes, I am. But it seems we have no choice but to go on. If all Merlin tells us is true ... and he has offered some strange proofs of his credentials!.. then we are engaged in something too important to run from." Rhea considered her words carefully. "I do not think we are important in ourselves, only what we represent as members of our race. Merlin said others will be involved in similar work in the Other places. I don't know. But I do believe that we shall not be asked to face more than we have the strength or courage to bear if we go into this with our whole hearts."

"Have you always felt like that?"

"For as long as I can remember. My grandmother taught me that and said we can bear far more than we think. Once, when I was terrified of going to the dentist, she told me to be brave. I said I couldn't be brave because I was scared. She sat me on her knees and explained that being brave didn't mean being without fear. Courage, she said, was doing the things that frighten you; there is no bravery involved in doing something you are not afraid of. It made sense and has stuck. I thought of her every time I had to catch a spider in Anna's room without cringing." Rhea smiled at the memory of her small daughter tucking up her feet in case the "'piders" bit her toes. "She was a wise old lady and her philosophy has helped me through some bad times too."

Alec saw straight to the heart of the last statement.

"It must have been very hard when you lost your husband. You miss him still?"

"It was devastating. A drunk driver hit his car and ran him off the road. Life felt very empty for a long time after that. Yes, I still miss him. He was a good husband and father and we had been best friends since college. We were happy together in a comfortable sort of way. It wasn't the grand passion I'd dreamed of as a girl, but we cared for each other deeply and built a good home for our daughter." Rhea sighed and shrugged her shoulders.

"It is hard to find the right way to describe what we had, without appearing to belittle it. I loved Mike very much, but I don't think we were ever really in love. Marriage just seemed to happen. Our life was very ordinary, very conventional." She laughed quietly and shook her head. "I know Mike would disapprove of my rather Bohemian lifestyle today and would certainly condemn Merlin as a fraud or a lunatic. Yet I feel more alive today than I ever have!"

Alec was treated to one of Rhea's luminous smiles and thought to himself that the late Michael Marchant had much to answer for. This extraordinary woman had so much more to offer than could be expressed while tied to a metaphorical kitchen sink.

"I have no regrets," Rhea continued as if she had developed Heilyn's talent for reading minds, "though there were many things I should have liked to have done. I have Anna, I was comfortable and content for twenty years. Now, though, I feel I would be frustrated by such a narrow existence.

"Grandma also taught me that nothing in life is ever wasted. Even the worst experiences can teach us something about ourselves or others if we take time to look for the lesson. Sometimes I think we wait too long to start looking and miss the opportunities we should have had, because we are wallowing in gloom or self-pity. Or maybe we are too afraid to upset the status quo and go out into unknown territory. Which brings me right back to Grandma and the dentist, doesn't it?"

She shook her head and met Alec's eyes.

"You shouldn't have let me run on like that! You are a very good listener, though! You managed not to look bored at all!"

"Don't underestimate yourself, Rhea. You have given me food for thought and some advice which I shall try and find the courage to take."

Alec reached out and plucked a rose from the bush beside the seat and placed it in Rhea's upturned hand, curling her fingers gently over the petals.

"Merlin has told us something of the dangers inherent in our task. Will you remember that I will be with you in whatever we have to face? I promise I will do all I can to keep you safe. I too am afraid and feel very much out of my depth, but I want to be there if you need me."

The words were stilted and awkward, but there was no mistaking the sincerity or warmth in his voice and Rhea was keenly aware of the effort it had cost the man to say these things. In an impulsive gesture of understanding she leaned closer and laid her hand against his cheek.

"Thank you Alec. That means a great deal to me." Her eyes misted with unshed tears as she felt Alec catch his breath at her touch. He took her face in his hands and kissed her gently on the lips.

A delighted chuckle broke the spell and Alec turned to find Heilyn perched on the wall behind them.

Chapter Seven

IN THE LIBRARY

"Will they do, Merlin?" asked Elizabeth. "Rhea I can understand. There is strength there and vision, something more too that I haven't quite fathomed yet. Jamie is still very young and seems to be treating it as some kind of adventure. My son, much as I love him, does not appear to fit the mould, in fact I would have said he was a complete sceptic. He has never shown any interest in anything otherworldly. His feet have been firmly on the ground for so long I was beginning to think he had taken root."

The tone was light, but there was real concern in her words. Of all those around him, Elizabeth was the only one in whom Merlin had confided for many years and so the only person who had any real grasp of the import of their venture.

"I agree with you, Rhea is special; it only remains for her to realise her potential. She seems to be the unifying agent in all this. Jamie is steady enough at heart. I shall not worry too much about him. He reminds me of some of Arthur's young men at the very beginning, when the world still seemed full of glory to them. Alec has a lot to learn about himself that he does not suspect. He has not believed before because has had no need, but he will not question the evidence put before him by people he knows and loves. I think Alec will prove to be the firm foundation upon which we will all depend.

What worries me most is the missing member of the company. I cannot see what is ahead and that is beginning to bother me."

"Perhaps you do not need to know yet. It is possible that events will show you the way without forcing the issue."

"I know, but it is so frustrating!" Merlin stood and paced the floor, his restlessness showing his concern more clearly than words. "I wondered if it could be Sabrina, but that doesn't feel quite right. I was afraid it might be you."

"My friend, I would give all in the service of the Light."

"I know. You always have." He looked with love at the fragile woman. "But I have no idea at all." He threw up his hands and turned to stare out of the window.

Elizabeth watched, willing her fading sight to last a little longer. Watching, she saw her friend's expression change from worry, through surprise and then to glee. He beckoned Elizabeth to his side.

"I told you Alec had a lot to learn about himself. I think he is enjoying his lessons, don't you? Working together is bound to bring them closer, the magic creates a bond." They watched as Alec took Rhea's face in his hands. "Would you mind, Beth?"

"My friend, nothing could please me more. She would be so good for him. I wonder if they have realised yet."

"Shall I tell them?" asked Jamie, joining the pair at the window and grinning from ear to ear, delighted at what he saw.

"Don't you dare, young man, or I'll turn you into a toad!" Jamie ducked the playful swipe aimed at his head.

"Can you do that, Merlin? The storybook kind of magic?"

"Some, lad. I can certainly turn *me* into a toad, so you shouldn't be much of a problem. I'll show you some time." Jamie's face lit up at this offhand promise, while Merlin's suddenly looked like thunder. "Now that," he snapped, "is one individual I would like to do something dreadful to!"

They followed his accusing finger to where Heilyn had appeared and to Jamie's eternal delight, Merlin vanished in the traditional puff of smoke, only to reappear directly in front of the laughing immortal. Heilyn evidently found much to amuse him in the torrent of threats his brother rained down upon him. Jamie, not wanting to miss the fun, sauntered out to eavesdrop on the one-sided conversation.

"...you will not interfere in this, at least. Time is a requirement for humans. This will take care of itself! No matter how clearly you may see!"

"You humans complicate even the simplest of things!" Heilyn sighed in mock innocence. "You know how it is, having been other than human yourself and you remember..."

"They are not rabbits!" the old man countered quickly.

"... and the doe..."

"Heilyn, enough." The calm command of Elizabeth's tone was unexpected and effective. Heilyn slid from his perch and bowed before the elegant figure.

"Lady, I give you greeting."

"Do you think you could stop tormenting Merlin for a little while and give us some advice?"

"How may I serve you?"

"I could make a few suggestions," muttered his brother.

"Both of you, behave yourselves, " Elizabeth chided, for all the world as if she were addressing a pair of naughty children, thought Alec and grinned. "Heilyn, we are concerned about the last member of our company. What can we do?"

"You are late with your question. I have already attended to the matter and the Bearer of Flame will be here when it is needful. Willingness is yet to be proved, but that is not my task."

"Why are you here, Heilyn? Is there some purpose to your visit, or were you just meddling?" Merlin inquired.

"A little of both perhaps, or perhaps both are the same, or maybe just for the pleasure of your company, brother mine." Mischief lit his eyes as Merlin grunted. "My mother sent this message: 'Heart of Earth, when the Beast awakens, remember that the Light will guide the blind through the shadows.' Don't ask me for explanations, Mother is bending the rules enough as it is." But the mage was already lost in contemplation of the strange words.

"Cernunnos called you Heart of Earth, Rhea," said Jamie. "Could the rest of the message relate to you, Elizabeth?"

"I don't know. I think I have no part in this. Heilyn?" There was no reply.

"He has gone, Mother." Alec took her hand and guided her to the seat, the fading light having robbed her of the last vestiges of sight. "Merlin, have you come up with anything?" The old man snapped out of his reverie,

"What? No, not yet. I think we need to have a look in the library. Mab would not give warning unless there was a real danger that we were unprepared to meet. That worries me. We have a little time, but none to waste." He turned to Elizabeth and took her hand. "My dear, we must go. We will keep in touch."

"Look after them, Merlin. I know this battle is greater than any one of us, but I shall not forgive you if you allow harm to come to them."

"I shall do all that is in my power to do," said Merlin in a curious echo of Alec's promise to Rhea. "Heilyn, if you're still eavesdropping, you might consider keeping Elizabeth company for a while," he added, addressing the empty air. A sparrow with an uncanny air of intelligence flew down from the branches and settled on Elizabeth's shoulder, tugging gently at her hair with its beak. "Convey my greetings and my gratitude to your mother when you return." Merlin bowed to the sparrow and Jamie wondered what on earth any observer would make of the scene.

The journey back to the Lodge was accomplished in near silence. Much had happened that needed to be understood and all were lost in their own thoughts.

Alec dropped Rhea at the cottage before continuing up the drive to the house. She was grateful for a little time alone, to assess the revelations of the day. She almost felt that she was watching a movie, the story compressed to fit the allotted running time, so much had been packed into the last three days. She had looked forward to starting her new job and had found herself, instead, catapulted into a strange new world, utterly alien to her experience but strangely familiar already.

Her own reactions puzzled her, she found it odd that she could accept so calmly her new status and converse with impossible creatures as if this were normality.

Rhea thought of her companions and the great strides into trust and friendship that had been taken in the short time since her arrival.

For Merlin she had great respect and affection. Only his own innate humanity, she decided, saved her from awe. Elizabeth, she felt, was a special case and she would have liked and admired the older woman whatever the circumstances of their meeting. Jamie was a dear and she was already very fond of him and Heilyn defied analysis. Cynicism, mockery and mirth, yet with an underlying feel of rightness that Rhea could not define.

What was she to make of Alec, though? From disapproval to protection, coldness to warmth all in a few short hours. Rhea was not a young woman and was unused to shying away from the truth. She realised quite clearly that Alec was attracted to her and was honest enough to admit the attraction was mutual and growing. What she didn't yet know was whether she was prepared to risk the contentment she had achieved since Mike's death by putting her happiness in someone else's hands.

Rhea was afraid to love and lose again. She was also concerned that the unnatural circumstances of their acquaintance were forcing an artificial intimacy that would not have developed in the normal course of events. Could any feelings be trusted in this situation? She did not know. All she knew was that his touch had felt like coming home.

Rhea showered and changed, choosing a jersey dress the colour of old roses. The softly tailored bodice made the most of her slender figure while the wide skirt fell in graceful folds to her knees and followed her movements as she walked. On impulse, she fastened the rose that Alec had given her at the shoulder of the dress before letting herself out of the cottage and into the night.

She had not thought to pick up a coat, the afternoon had been warm and she was unused to the Yorkshire weather. Mrs Long, meeting her in the hallway of the Lodge told her that the gentlemen were still in the library and she was to join them there,

"There's a good fire going in there, which you'll be glad of. You look fair nithered, lass. Still, I suppose you get different weather down south." The tone was mildly condescending. Mrs Long evidently thought 'down south' as foreign a place as Australia. The housekeeper let Rhea into the library and withdrew in the general direction of the kitchen.

Her arrival was greeted absently by Merlin who was immersed in a large and tattered volume which looked as if it held as much dust as it did paper. Alec turned immediately as she entered, his smile as welcoming as the fire he was tending. Jamie rose from the pile of paperbacks on the floor and cleared a place for her to sit.

"You are a sight for sore eyes, Rhea. I'm so glad you're here." Rhea was a little surprised at this enthusiastic greeting, but the compliment was rather spoilt by his next remark, "Now you've come, perhaps we can eat. I'm starved."

"You are always starving, my boy," said Merlin, eyes twinkling in the firelight. "Here you sit, surrounded by centuries of rare knowledge, enough to feed your soul for a lifetime and all you can think of is your stomach." The old man shook his head, his lips twitching with suppressed mirth. Rhea was glad to see that he had regained his sense of humour. "Run along and tell Mrs Long we will eat as soon as she is ready."

Jamie ran off with alacrity to do as he was told and Merlin bent back to his research. Rhea could think of nothing to say to Alec so she fell back on asking for a translation of the housekeeper's remark.

"Nithered means really cold," he explained. "I've never known where it comes from. There is still a lot of the old Yorkshire dialect in use; even the youngsters use it without giving it a second thought. I don't suppose you'd know what a ginnel is either? Any child will tell you and yet you'd probably have to use a whole sentence to define it."

"What is a ginnel? I've never heard it before."

"It's a narrow alley or footpath, usually running behind houses. There are many in the West Riding." Alec grinned, "I had to use a whole phrase too."

Rhea answered his smile with one of her own,

"And a Riding?"

"It means a third part, a 'thirding'. Yorkshire is divided into North, East and West Ridings, each with its own distinct character, almost as if they were separate counties. York is the capital, standing where the three counties meet, the Ainsty."

"And are all Yorkshiremen as proud of their heritage?"

"Oh yes," he replied." Meet one abroad and ask him where he comes from and he won't say England, but Yorkshire. We are as proud of our birthright as any Londoner"

"And southerners?"

"There is an old saying round her. Many people will still quote it when asked, but really I think we tend to treat anyone not from our own neck of the woods with a mixture of amused tolerance and pity them for not being Yorkshire born themselves."

Rhea was aware that she was being teased and found it surprising, coming from Alec. This was quite a different man from the serious and distant man she had first met.

"Are you going to tell her what the saying is?" Merlin inquired. The old man too was gratified by the change in his friend and was far too wise not to be able to guess the cause.

"She's a southerner herself, she might take offence," Alec pleaded.

"I'll take offence if you don't!"

"Well, don't say I didn't warn you. 'Southern born and southern bred, strong in body, weak in head.' Present company excepted of course," said he, ducking the cushions that Rhea and the elderly Welshman both threw at him laughing.

"Oddly," said Rhea, "we have a similar saying…it goes 'Yorkshire born…'"

Jamie and Mr Long returned at that moment to say that dinner would be served in five minutes. Jamie demanded an immediate explanation for the attack upon his friend, regretting having missed the fun. The sergeant-major eyed them sternly and commented that they were 'a bit old for 'aving lannigans when their soup was going cold'. Alec caught Rhea's eye and they both burst out laughing, to which Mrs Long replied,

"Humph."

Dinner was a lively meal, but by nine the four were back in the library with their coffee, sifting through the piles of books for some clue to the nature of their next challenge. It was Rhea, skimming through a slim volume of local legends who found the first reference to a beast in Trollers Gill.

The article said that the rocky valley had been named after the trolls of Norse myth, imported by early invaders. These creatures of cave and stone were said to roll boulders into the gill, thus explaining the mass of rocks on the valley floor.

There was a faded photo, showing a deep cleft between two hills, littered with great chunks of limestone following the course of a dry stream bed. At the top of the vale was a rugged slope, remnant of an ancient waterfall which closed the valley on its third side.

Rhea did not like the idea that there was only one way in or out of the place where she had to go and face her unknown adversary. She was none too happy about the possibility of meeting trolls either and skimmed the rest of the page in search of information. The article said nothing more about trolls, but did mention, without explanation, another creature.

"Do you know anything about the Barguest?"

"Why, have you found something?" Merlin put aside his book and gave his attention to Rhea, who read out the passage to the three men. Merlin considered the tale before replying. "The trolls are an obvious problem. I guessed they were the 'stone giants' and I think I have found a way to deal with them. They are alarming, but rather stupid. I had not considered the possibility of the Barguest, however. It explains the danger we were warned of."

"I have heard of it, but put it down as just another legend," said Alec with his wry smile. "But we seem to be walking with legends today. Tales tell that the Barguest is an enormous dog, as big as a calf and with fiery eyes the size of saucers."

Mrs Long had come in as Alec spoke to collect the coffee cups,

"The Barguest? Aye, that's right. My granddad used to tell the old stories when I were a lass. They say it means death to look in its eyes unless there's running water between you and there's nowt as can be done about it. Used to scare me feckless whenever I saw a dog's footprint in the mud. It's a shame the old stories are being forgotten. I sometimes think there's more to some on 'em than we know. Now. Professor, if you've done with me, I'm off home. The dogs are in the kitchen for the night."

Jamie held the door while she swept out, bidding her goodnight.

"Good night, God bless, Mr Jamie. Don't be keeping Mrs Marchant up nattering too long now, she's not looking too bright."

Alec had been watching Rhea and was inclined to agree with her. The fair skin had lost all trace of colour and Alec could see that she was beginning to realise that dealing with the Barguest was going to be her responsibility. A wave of impotent anger shook him, knowing that he could neither take her place nor protect her. Damn Merlin for bringing her into danger! Yet the ultimate choice was hers and he could only admire the courage with which she faced the ordeal. Her voice was steady as she spoke,

"So I have to prevail against the trolls and the Barguest. Why Merlin? What is the goal?"

"I believe you will be led to a thing of great power, should you succeed. Long ago, in the youth of Man, it is told that a great civilisation grew up on the island of Ruta. The tale was ancient even when I was a boy. Yes, Jamie," he nodded in response to the glowing expression on the boy's face, "today we call it Atlantis.

"The legends are as near the truth as we will ever know. At their height they had great knowledge of the tides of power in the Earth and reverence for the world which gave them shelter. However, a corrupt faction of the priesthood, product of a decaying civilisation, meddled, in their vanity, with forces beyond their control and provoked a catastrophe which laid waste to their cities and decimated their people. Some few were untouched by the folly and, seeing the direction their brothers had taken, sent out messengers to find new lands where a few of their race might take refuge and preserve their bloodline and wisdom.

"With these few were sent artefacts of power, forged by the priesthood to be vessels of Light. The remnants of Atlantis were the founders of Egyptian wisdom and were behind the birth of civilisations in the Americas. Certainly the megalithic people and builders of our own pyramids shared the wisdom and knowledge of the lost land."

"I didn't know we'd ever had pyramids in Britain?"

"Oh yes, Jamie. There is Silbury Hill, the largest man made mound in Europe. You have only to look at it to be struck by the shape. The Tynwald, Merlin's Mount near Marlborough and no, I don't know why it got its name, nothing to do with me at all. They both resemble the step pyramids of Saqqara or South America. Even Glastonbury Tor may have its inspiration in Atlantis.

"Anyway, to return to the story, these artefacts were not wholly of this world and drew their power from many sources. Every so often, events in our history have called upon a few to wield the power held within these things. Some were brought to our islands. They have been remade many times over the millennia in many forms.

"In Arthur's day there was the sword, the shield, the cup and the staff. When Arthur passed, the Lady of Avalon reclaimed them and withdrew them from the world, taking their essence and forging them into swords, way ahead of the technology of the time, with a little help from some of my family.

"At some time in the distant past the power was separated into its component parts to protect mankind from its abuse. The idea was that no one man was strong enough or wise enough to wield that amount of power alone. The swords now represent the symbolic elements, Air, Earth, Fire and Water. Together they call forth the element that binds the threads of the universe.

"We approach the dawn of a new age for humakind. The precession of the equinoxes is taking us into the Aquarian age. The hippies of the sixties were not entirely misguided. Our task is to bring the symbols of the elements together to herald in that New Age. The nature of this new beginning will be shaped by our success or failure. The future of the soul of Man is in our care and we must not fail."

The magnitude of their task shocked the three listeners. The quest was worth any price they might be required to pay and they felt small and insignificant despite their given role. It was once again Rhea who voiced the question in all their thoughts,

"Who are we to be chosen for this? We are neither warriors nor magicians; we have nothing special to bring to this."

"It is not mine to judge why. I am a servant of the Light and I obey the prompting of my heart, asking guidance of the One. But I think you were chosen because you represent your race and have the innate qualities required to succeed. You will have to take it on trust, but I think you can safely believe that someone 'up there' knows what they are at."

The kindly tone and simple words reassured them more than anything else Merlin could have offered.

"Think about this; we have worked together for a very short time and yet have fitted together like the pieces of a jigsaw. The magic of the quest will enhance this relationship and empathy will grow whether you will it or not. Rhea is a newcomer, yet do you not feel as close to her as if you had known her for years?"

The two men concurred.

"Rhea, have you not found it so too?"

"Yes, in the few days I've been here, which seems like no time and a lifetime, I have learned to care for you all." The admission took courage and she sat, straight as the sword she hoped to wield.

"Accept it and do not worry that the feeling will vanish when the work is done. Love is never a gift to be rejected, wherever it is given." Ancient sorrow clouded the old man's gaze and Rhea thought of Nimue and the ring she wore. "Follow your hearts, my children. Joy is not forbidden."

There was comfort in Merlin's words. Jamie was reluctant to disturb the peace which now pervaded the room, but it was growing late and his curiosity had to be satisfied.

"How are we going to deal with the trolls, Merlin? If any of the tales are true I wouldn't fancy Rhea's chances against them." In reply, the familiar chuckle.

"A little illusion should take care of them, but unless Heilyn can be persuaded to help, it will keep me fully occupied. I should be able to fool them; I just need to work out the best way to do it."

"Is it true that they turn to stone in sunlight?" asked Alec, who had, at least, read some of the right books it seemed.

"Perfect, Alec!" Merlin almost bounced with glee. "I'll give them a sunrise!"

"You can do that?" Jamie's incredulous awe was a sight to behold and Merlin further delighted him by folding his hands as if in prayer, only to part them, revealing a tiny landscape, sheltering in his palms.

As they watched the horizon behind the miniature hills began to brighten and the sun, no larger than a child's marble, rose in a haze of pink and gold. Birds circled between the fingertips and trees waved their branches in the breeze. Merlin allowed them to marvel at his skill for a few moments more before closing his hands to disperse the illusion.

"I'll have to work on a larger scale of course," he said, trying to appear nonchalant, but evidently pleased with their reaction. "Once I locate their cave, I'll create an illusion to cover the entrance and with any luck I'll be able to hold it there long enough for Rhea to pass in safety. Jamie, I will need your help. Alec, you will accompany Rhea."

"And the Barguest?" prompted Alec. Merlin's face clouded again.

"I shall have to give some thought to this. There are some lines of research to follow, legends of a black dog, similar to the Barguest, in Norfolk. I may find something to help us. Mab's message may contain some clue we have missed. For the time being, I would suggest we all get some sleep and come at the problem fresh in the morning."

Chapter Eight

THE HAND OF THE FAE

The night air was cold and Alec again draped his jacket across Rhea's shoulders as he escorted her back to the cottage. They walked quietly, side by side, each waiting for the other to open the conversation, neither knowing where to begin. Before them in the gloom, a ghostly shape materialised. Rhea gasped and turned to Alec in fear, and he held her close against his body, suddenly ready to fight all the demons their nebulous Enemy could conjure to protect the woman in his arms. The shadowy creature continued its approach.

"Baaaa."

Rhea laughed. It took Alec a few seconds longer to grasp the situation then he too began to laugh. The stray ram regarded the two humans and cocked its head to one side. They were clinging to each other for support in their mirth, a welcome release after the tensions of the day. Alec wiped Rhea's eyes with his handkerchief and the tender gesture seemed to alter the atmosphere between them. Alec released her and stepped away.

"Come on, let's get you home." He started towards the cottage again, Rhea following in his wake. Had either of them been looking they might have seen an expression akin to frustration cross the blunt features of the ram.

Rhea turned the key in the lock and said goodnight to Alec, but as she opened the door to step inside, the ram charged. Head down, it ran full tilt towards Alec, the curved horns glinting wickedly in the starlight.

Not stopping to think, Rhea grabbed Alec by the arm and pulled him inside, slamming the door behind them. A crash on the heavy oak door proved that her action had been timely.

"Thanks," said Alec. "I'll give him a couple of minutes to calm down then I'll make a dash for the car. It's most unusual for a ram to charge unless it feels threatened. I can't understand what has got into that one." He looked around as if searching for something. "Do you have my jacket there?"

"Oh dear, don't you have it? We must have dropped it in the rush to get in."

"Not to worry, it can only be just outside. My car keys are in the pocket though."

"Would you like a drink while we wait?" she asked.

"Better not, thanks. I'll be off in a couple of minutes." Alec peered through the letter box to check on the ram. "The damn thing is sitting on my coat!" He was laughing now. "It looks like it's lying in wait to ambush me!" Rhea took his place at the aperture and was forced to agree. The ram looked in no hurry to move.

"I'll phone the Lodge and get Jamie to bring the dogs over to round him up." She dialled the number and let the phone ring, eventually the metallic voice of the answering machine cut in and she was obliged to leave a message. "They're probably asleep already."

"It's okay. Sheep are not vindictive animals. It will soon lose interest and wander off." Again he checked on the animal. "Still sitting on my jacket! I can't go anywhere till it moves, I'm afraid!"

"In that case," said Rhea, "you may as well have that drink. What can

I get you?"

"I'd love a coffee, if you really don't mind." He sat down on the sofa as Rhea went into the kitchen. She reappeared several minutes later to find her guest asleep on the couch. She took advantage of the situation to have a good look at the man.

He was tall, she knew, as she came just to his shoulder. The dark hair was streaked with grey and the skin tanned by the wind and sun. The brow was high and wide, unmarked in sleep by the worry lines which gave him an almost perpetual frown when awake. The slightly aquiline nose and square, stubborn jaw gave the face strength and character.

It was an attractive face, Rhea thought, one to trust. Yet in sleep there was a curious vulnerability about it. She considered waking him, but the recalcitrant sheep was still at its post and seemed to be settled for the night, so she brought a blanket from the bedroom and covered him, switched off the light and went to bed. She found it strange trying to sleep knowing Alec was only a few feet away, but the stresses of the day eventually caught up with her and she drifted into dream.

It was around two in the morning when Alec was woken by the sounds of distress coming from the bedroom. Disoriented for a moment, he wondered where he was, then realisation came and he was on his feet.

Rhea seemed to be crying in her sleep and the sound tugged at his heart. His resolve snapped at a particularly heart rending cry of denial and he pushed open the door quietly and approached the sleeping figure. As she cried out again he leaned down and shook her gently.

Still distressed and more than half asleep, she clung to him, clutching at his shirt. Alec held her close, stroking her hair and whispering soothing noises to ease her fear. Rhea laid her head on his shoulder with a soft sigh.

"What the hell," thought Alec. Kicking off his shoes, he lifted his legs onto the bed and lay down beside Rhea, holding her close and finally watching her sink into an easy sleep.

With her head cradled on his chest, he took her hand in his and held it against the bare skin of his throat, revelling in her nearness and the feel of her. Utterly content, he dropped a soft kiss on the brown curls and fell asleep.

Had Alec known that the ram had long since vanished, he would have left before the nightmare had gripped Rhea. As it turned out, they spent the night in each other's arms. Which was precisely what the erstwhile ram had intended.

Some while earlier, the ram had dissolved into a shimmer of air and had reappeared in his more usual guise. Heilyn was well pleased with the strategy he had employed to bring the two together with no more waste of time.

A flick of his fingers created the simulacrum of a second ram out of thin air, which he carefully arranged on Alec's jacket. He surveyed his handiwork with a critical eye, adding a finishing touch before sauntering off in the direction of the Lodge, leaving the illusory ram chewing placidly on a sleeve.

Jamie had gone to bed as soon as the others had left and Merlin had followed shortly afterwards. He was still considering the problem of the Barguest as he undressed and threw his clothes in a heap on the chair.

"Not a pretty sight, Merlin! Must you look so old, dear one?" Merlin made a lunge for a dressing gown to cover his nakedness, only to find an intruder sitting on it, employing very similar tactics to Heilyn's sheep. He retreated behind the inadequate cover provided by a small towel and swore graphically.

"Aren't you pleased to see me, dearest?" The lithe figure reclining on the bed stretched provocatively, trapping the dressing gown ever more firmly beneath her. Long black hair billowed across the bedspread in curling tendrils and the diaphanous gown left little doubt that most men would be very pleased to see her. Merlin bowed with considerable dignity, holding tightly to his towel.

"Madam, I would be far happier to see you if you were seeing rather less of me."

"Why do you wear that thing, Merlin?"

"The towel?"

A ripple of laughter.

"No, the flesh. It is rather shabby looking and bits of it look as if they are too big for you. It displeases me."

"It is comfortable and I'm used to it," said Merlin defensively.

"Do something about it for me, dear one," the perfect nose wrinkled in distaste. "It wobbles when you speak." A smile of impure mischief lit the golden eyes. "Would you like me to handle it?"

Merlin bit back the retort which sprang to mind and decided this was one battle he was unlikely to win. He shrugged and the air around him rippled, leaving a youthful figure in place of the elderly mage. This was the Merlin who had changed the fate of Britain. Tall and lean, with shoulder length hair and rippling muscle.

"Better, Mab?" he asked in the light baritone of youth. Mab took her time inspecting the new form, her eyes lingering like a caress on his skin.

Merlin blushed. All over.

"Infinitely better, dear one." Her eyes narrowed to predatory slits and she smiled, revealing a glimpse of perfect white teeth. "Especially as you forgot the towel…" Merlin glanced down in confusion and snapped his fingers, protecting his modesty with a long white robe edged in blue.

"Spoilsport!" laughed the lady.

"To what do I owe the honour of your presence, Madam?"

"So formal, Merlin. I wonder why?" The lady wriggled a little, her every move and word infused with a laughing invitation. "Heilyn gave me your message; I thought you might like to thank me personally." The promise in the low voice would have tempted a lesser man beyond endurance. Merlin however, had centuries of practice with which to defend himself.

"I do thank you, although I don't pretend to understand your words." Mab abandoned her game with a sigh of regret.

"You will, or rather, she will when the time comes. You know I'm not supposed to interfere, so I can't be any clearer without breaking the rules. I won't do that."

"No, just bend them a little."

"Of course!" she laughed. "I always have."

She stood and the raven hair cascaded to her knees, a more modest covering than her gown. She was perfect, the answer to a man's wildest fantasies. Merlyn felt desire stirring as he had not for many a year. He gave himself up to the feeling for a few moments, enjoying the remembered sensation, before resolutely quashing the thoughts rather than follow where they inevitably led.

Mab tracked his emotions with a knowing smile of amusement and regret. He had never given in to her appeal, which of course made it more exciting to tease him. Merlin sighed and pulled himself together.

"You are truly magnificent, my lady." He took her hand and carried it to his lips.

"You have always been a gentleman, Merlin. A pity. Are the two younger ones as bad?"

Merlin chose to ignore the implications of that remark.

"Alec is a gentleman, yes. And Jamie is young enough to be your son." Mab indeed looked in her mid-thirties, a rich maturity with a hint of springtime.

"You forget, Merlin. Even you are young enough for that." She withdrew her hand and turned from him. "I follow my own agenda, dear one. You may not command me in this." Merlin felt a stab of concern for his friends. "There are forces at work here beyond your ken. Leave it at that, Merlin. I shall not cause harm." Merlin began to speak, and she laid a finger on his lips, tracing the curve of his mouth slowly. "It is not permitted to ask more. Be content that I serve more than my own pleasure in this." The tone was both regal and gentle and Merlin knew he had been given an oblique warning.

There was subtle shift in the atmosphere of the room and Merlin looked up.

"Come in, my son," said the lady. "You are not interrupting anything, he still won't play." Heilyn crystallised from the air, looking so full of mischief that Merlin was immediately suspicious. The laughing eyes took in Merlin's rejuvenated form and his mother's attire and the eyebrows arched in quizzical humour.

"Say one word and I strangle you!" growled the mage before Heilyn had a chance to open his mouth. "What have you been up to?" Heilyn sauntered over to the window and looked out into the night.

"Make up your mind, dear brother. I can't answer if I can't speak."

"You know perfectly well what I meant. What are you doing here tonight? I haven't seen you in half a hundred years and this is the third time you've turned up today. You're looking far too pleased with yourself and I don't trust you in this mood. What have you been up to?"

"What do you think, mother? Should we tell him? He's getting very annoyed. I wouldn't want him to have a heart attack, you know." Merlin raised his eyes to the heavens in exasperation.

"Please, Heilyn," asked Merlin, the tone deliberately calm through gritted teeth, "tell me why you are here tonight?" The small entity shared a glance with his mother who nodded almost imperceptibly.

"Before he tells you, dear one, know that he but does my bidding in this and with your father's knowledge. Events move too fast and human scruples have no place in this. They have to feel easy with each other and we knew you would not act. We cannot permit uncertainty."

"They? Heilyn?"

"Your lovebirds are spending the night together." His tone was smug and his footwork nimble as he dodged behind his mother, waiting for the inevitable explosion.

"What! How in the name of all the gods did you achieve that? I specifically told you to leave them alone!"

Merlin was pacing the floor, his face flushed with anger. Mab waited a few moments, allowing him to vent his spleen by threatening all manner of atrocities to be visited on his brother. When she spoke, all the command of the Otherworld was in her voice,

"Peace, Merlin! It was required. Heed me. They would have sniffed around each other like a pair of dogs had we not intervened. Heilyn was instructed to give them a gentle nudge that is all."

"It would have been more than a nudge if they hadn't run so fast!" chuckled Heilyn. He described the encounter with great gusto and even Merlin was laughing by the end of his recital. The mental image of the sheep chewing away at the jacket finally proved Merlin's undoing and he sat down, wiping his eyes with his sleeve.

"So, where are they now?" he asked finally, when his voice was steady enough to speak.

"Last time I checked they were cuddled up together on the bed, fast asleep. I doubt if we've pushed them too hard though, he's still fully clothed."

Heilyn sounded vaguely disappointed, but his brother was glad to know his friends were to be allowed at least some leeway in their romance.

"I have to admit that since I introduced them, the hope that they would be together has not been too far from my mind. They could be so good for each other. Heilyn, for once you have my apologies, brother. I approve." The merry immortal pantomimed extreme shock and fell backwards on the bed. "Don't push it!" growled Merlin.

"They were made for each other, dearest. They have waited a lifetime for each other without knowing. This was preordained." Even Merlin was awed by this pronouncement, so seldom did the gods tamper with human destiny in this way. "Have you not seen how well the woman fits the nature of the weapon she is to bear? She is of Earth, warm and practical, the mother, life-giver. And does the man, with his quick intellect, not epitomise the qualities of Air?"

"The Windlord, yes, it fits of course. The two opposites, the halves made whole. Yes, I see it now. Then, their own happiness depends also on our success."

"Their very lives depend upon it," replied the Queen of Faery, "so closely are they and their weapons linked. We cannot...."

The bedroom door opened and Jamie burst in. He took a swift look around the room and fastened on the one familiar face,

"Heilyn, where is Merlin, there's something wrong. Alec's car is still parked outside and it is nearly half past three."

"Everything is under control, Jamie," answered Merlin. Heilyn sat back and prepared to enjoy the encounter.

"Who are you?"

"It's me, lad! Oh bother!" Jamie's eyes widened as Merlin, having quite forgotten his altered appearance, shimmered back to his accustomed form. He presented an astonishing spectacle, as he again forgot the towel, a mistake he immediately regretted as a silvery peal of laughter rang out. He instantly created a bathrobe for himself and pulled the belt tight, glaring at his tormentors and daring them to pass further comment on his attire, or lack of it.

"Her Majesty was offended by his wrinkles," offered Heilyn, by way of explanation.

"Well, dear one, there were so many of them. And in such funny places," the lady apologised.

"Can we leave my wrinkles out of this?"

"I liked it so much better when you did," countered the queen. Merlin gave up.

Jamie could not drag his eyes from the fascinating creature who confronted him. She was more beautiful than a summer morning, a radiant being, proud as an empress and yet as soft and warm as a kitten, fragile as a butterfly's wing. Merlin had seen this reaction before and gritted his teeth. Nothing in all his armoury of magic could defend Jamie now. The boy would have to work this one out for himself.

"Won't you present him to me, Merlin?"

"Majesty," the old man complied, hoping that the lady's identity would help the mesmerised boy. "May I present James Dixon, who is to bear the weapon of Water? Jamie, this is Mab, Queen of Faery and Heilyn's mother, of whom I have spoken." Any hope that this final, pointed reminder would help guard the boy was dashed, as Mab held out her hand to Jamie and he raised it reverently to his lips.

"Sweet boy. What tales has Merlin told you, I wonder?"

"Only that you were beautiful. I thought a bard such as he would have drawn nearer to the truth, but I doubt if any words could do you justice."

"Merlin, where have you been hiding this one? He reminds me of Bedwyr. I liked Bedwyr." Merlin never understood how she could put so many levels of meaning into a seemingly innocent phrase. Jamie shook his head slightly as if to bring the world back into focus. Thinking seemed hard work.

"Alec! Merlin, Alec's car is still here, is something wrong?"

"No, lad, everything is as it should be, or so Heilyn informs me."

"But why is the car still here? I got up because I heard voices. I thought he must be with you. Where is he?" Heilyn, noted Merlin, was enjoying all this immensely.

"Yes, Alec is here, but he isn't here." Not surprisingly, Jamie couldn't grasp the meaning of this. He looked at Mab and Heilyn, wondering to what uncanny realm his friend had been sent. Merlin sighed. The boy would have to be told. "Alec is spending the night with Rhea. There was a slight accident and he couldn't get away."

"Accident? With the car? Is he okay?"

"Not the car, no. With a sheep."

"A sheep?" Jamie found the explanation harder to follow by the second. Merlin was making no sense at all and Heilyn was rolling with mirth.

"Yes, Jamie. A sheep. That's what I said. Snap out of it lad. You don't have to repeat everything I say."

"Sorry, Merlin. I don't understand at all."

"Don't look so sheepish, Jamie," chuckled Heilyn. Three pairs of eyes turned on the merry immortal and he buried his head in the pillows to stifle his laughter.

"Listen carefully. Alec was ambushed by a sheep when he walked Rhea back to the cottage. The sheep ate his jacket and his car keys were in the pocket. He had to stay at Rhea's as the sheep wouldn't let him get out. Now, is that clear?"

"No, Merlin. Not at all. It doesn't make any sense. Why would a sheep attack Alec and eat his jacket?"

"Because, lad, that is the twisted way in which Heilyn's mind works." The wheels were now in motion and understanding began to filter through the fog in Jamie's mind. A slow smile spread across his face as the implications of the trap became clear. He looked at the shaking bundle on the bed and grinned.

"Nice work, Heilyn. But you'll have Alec on the rampage if he ever finds out." A veritable scream of hysterical giggles greeted this remark.

"Rampage, *rampage!*"

Mab, a smile curling the corners of her own delicious mouth, regarded the quivering heap.

"I think I'll take him home, Merlin. He is beginning to get a little out of hand." She turned to Jamie and ran one nail, almost gently, down the side of his face. "I shall see you again, sweet boy." Then she and Heilyn were gone and silence returned to the room, broken only by the thudding of Jamie's heart.

"You can't tell Alec or Rhea about any of this, you realise."

"Of course not, Merlin. I'll be as surprised as you like. But I must say, I'm glad Heilyn has helped them along a bit. Neither of them seemed to know where to start. They're made for each other, you know." With this surprising insight, Jamie yawned and took himself back to bed.

Rhea was the first to wake next morning. She eased back to consciousness with her head still pillowed on Alec's chest, the steady beat of his heart a counterpoint to the ticking of the clock. His chest rose and fell with each breath beneath her cheek as she awoke, touched once again by his concern for her and his gentleness. She recalled the nightmares through a haze of fear, great black beasts with burning eyes that devoured her. She also remembered safety and comfort found once more in Alec's arms.

A great and empty well of loneliness was filled for Rhea as she lay. The simple gift of touch was a wonder as she gently moved her fingers to curl around his neck, holding herself closer to him, as if she had the right, hardly daring to move lest he wake and move away.

There was such beauty in the moment and it moved Rhea deeply, a thing so fragile and so long missed that tears welled unbidden to her eyes. Rhea knew she cried too readily these days, but this, this was precious. Pain and longing, loneliness and loss, all were eclipsed by the glow of a moment.

"Why the tears, Rhea?" His voice was as soft as his touch on her hand and she could not answer. How could she explain all that his nearness meant?

He moved to slide his arm from beneath her and the lack of contact with him was as great a bereavement as any she had known. But he didn't move away after all. He propped himself on one arm, his body still touching hers, and looked down at her gravely. She wanted to turn away, to close her eyes and hide but Alec's eyes would not let her go.

He traced the path of her tears with one fingertip and smoothed the tousled hair away from her face.
"You look so lovely this morning. Can't you tell me what's wrong? I don't want to upset you." Rhea could still find no words, but managed a watery smile. "I should go. I didn't like to think of you alone and frightened." He began to disengage himself slowly, reluctantly it seemed. Rhea took her courage in both hands and finally spoke,

"No Alec, don't go, please." Greatly daring, she raised her hand to his face. He leaned in to her touch, eyes closed, and kissed the palm that caressed his mouth. She slid her hand into his hair and pulled him closer. His eyes searched hers in wonder and found what they sought there. His own hands were lost in the silky curls as he let himself be drawn down. The kiss was gentle, hesitant, each savouring the touch and taste of the other, as they embarked upon a voyage of endless discovery.

Alec felt his chest tighten and his breath came rapidly as he kissed her lips, her brow and the closed eyes.

"Dear God, Rhea, do you know what you're doing to me?" For answer Rhea only drew him closer, her hands now sliding inside his shirt to find the smooth skin of his back. Her touch was electric and Alec rolled away and sat on the edge of the bed, head in hands. "I'm so sorry, Rhea. That was unforgivable of me."

His voice was raw with emotion and Rhea, sure now of her own feelings and as confident as Eve, came to stand before him. The window at her back limned her slender form in light. The man before her was strung so tightly she knew she had to break down his barriers once and for all.

"Alec." He did not lift his head, merely shook it slightly. Rhea knelt before him so her face was level with his. "Alec, the only unforgivable act would be to leave me now."

She spoke softly and there was no answer from the man, who seemed to be wrestling with himself. She reached forward and began to open the remaining buttons on his shirt, amazed at her own temerity. He raised his head and looked at Rhea, hope stealing into his face but still holding himself tightly in check.

"Rhea?" A world of meaning in a single word. She laid her hands on his chest, feeling the tightness of muscle and smooth skin, until he was trembling beneath her hands. She laughed, the sound coming from a well-spring of joy.

"Oh love, I have waited for you for so long." The man she had met but a few days ago needed no further sign. With a strangled sob he crushed her to him, burying his face in her neck and he wept.

She held him thus, kneeling upright between his thighs until the storm abated, stroking the grizzled hair with one hand, caressing the nape of his neck with the other, taking his weight until he was calm.

"What time is it?" he asked, kissing her throat, oh so gently, and letting his hands stray over the soft skin of her shoulders.

"A little after six, I think." Rhea replied.

"You can't be very comfortable on the floor. Let me help you up." He lifted her easily in his arms and held her like this a moment, looking down at her face, before laying her gently on the bed. "I really ought to go. They will be waking at the Lodge soon and the car is still outside." In spite of his words he showed no sign of leaving.

"Does it matter? I think they might notice anyway," Rhea felt alive, unbelievably alive. She didn't care if the whole world knew her feelings as long as Alec knew. "We're not children, love." She sat up and, leaning close to him, slid her hands once more beneath the thin fabric of his shirt, easing it over his shoulders and down his arms until it fell unnoticed to the floor.

Rhea could not believe that she was behaving like this. It had never been this way with Mike. He would have been shocked had she tried to seduce him. Lights out and only the comfort of closeness to remember in the night. Not this fierce joy at the taste of his skin on her lips nor the glory of feeling him tremble at her touch.

And Alec was trembling as he, in turn, slid the straps of her nightdress from her shoulders and the silky stuff slid to her waist. His hands found the small of her back and pulled her hard against him, trapping her hands against his chest. His breath came in ragged gasps as he tried to retain some semblance of restraint, but years of rigid self-denial and control were being ground to nothing under the rising tide of passion.

"Rhea, are you sure?" Rhea drew away to look him directly in the eyes, smiling, incandescent in the golden light of morning.

"Yes, love. Very sure." The last of the barriers crumbled as he reached for her and she drew him down onto the bed.

Chapter Nine

REMEMBER ME

Jamie and Merlin were just finishing breakfast when the dogs gave warning of someone entering the Lodge. The young man looked questioningly at his mentor. Merlin was fiddling with his napkin and felt as fidgety as a mother hen. It was so important to him that Alec and Rhea should find some degree of happiness and to find it together would be wonderful for them. He knew Rhea's story, far more than she had told him. Alec had worried him for a long time. It was not right that a man such as he should have cut himself off from joy so young. Solitude had become a habit with him and to Merlin he had seemed only half alive, his heart barricaded against intrusion. Alec was not a man to love lightly. If he gave himself, the gift would be complete and it would take a special woman to stand against the torrent and yet have the depth to give him what he needed.

The door to the dining room opened to admit them. Merlin scanned their faces, trying to read there what he wanted to know. They were smiling and at ease together and there was something more there too. With a mental shrug, Merlin breached the rules of etiquette to read their hearts and was both awed and humbled by what he found there. He stood to greet them, tears pricking his eyes.

"Good morning, my children." Love and pride warmed the simple greeting and Rhea's understanding smile lit the room. Merlin did not know what to say and sought refuge in normality. "Would you like some coffee? Have you eaten yet?"

"Coffee is fine, thanks," replied Rhea. She looked at Alec, her heart in her eyes. An almost imperceptible nod answered her unspoken question. "We had breakfast earlier." So, thought the old man, they were not going to hide.

"I shall have to go home shortly anyway," added Alec. "I need to change." He indicated his crumpled clothing. Jamie couldn't resist,

"You look like you slept in them." He was rewarded by a kick on the shin from the old gentleman. "What are the plans for today?"

"I'd like you to have a run down to the library, Jamie," said Merlin. "There is a list of references I need checking on my desk. Alec, what are your plans?"

"I have to run into Leeds to see Sabrina. I'll be back around twelve, so if you don't need Rhea here, I thought I'd take her down to the river and call in on Mother before tonight."

"I'd like to paint this morning," offered Rhea, "unless there is anything I can do for you here? I've hardly been earning my keep so far!"

"My dear Rhea, the work we are engaged on is far more important than the job you were engaged to do! Your paintings are valuable in both cases though and I think you should paint whenever you can. It will do you good and the results may be interesting." Jamie choked on his coffee, his quick mind reading more into the old man's statement than was intended. Alec stood up and looked uncertainly at his love.

"I have to go or I won't get back in time." Jamie could not resist one last gentle dig at his friend,

"Is it warm outside, Alec? You're not wearing your jacket."

"A sheep chewed a hole in it last night."

"How on earth did it do that? Didn't you notice?" Jamie's expression was bland, but his shins would be black and blue by teatime.

"Idiot. I wasn't wearing it. It's a long story." Alec and Rhea shared a look that told a story of its own. Till that moment, Jamie had regarded their budding romance lightly, though with approval, but the open adoration on Alec's face and the joy Rhea exuded made his flippant remarks seem childish and misplaced. He abandoned any further attempt to milk the situation, envying them their happiness and union, but glad beyond words that two people he cared for had come together in love.

"I'll walk you to the car, Alec. I'll be ready by noon." Rhea slipped her hand through Alec's arm and they left the room together.

Merlin and Jamie watched through the window as they stood together by the car. They saw Alec take the upturned face in his hands and kiss Rhea with infinite tenderness and felt the reluctance of their parting. A sniff from behind the alerted them to a third presence in the room.

"Eeh, that's a bonny sight." Mrs Long was drying her eyes on a corner of her pinafore. "Ah've seen Mr Alec grow up from a bairn and after t' way that trollop dumped him, Ah nivver thowt Ah'd see him this suited." Jamie grinned. He had often noted the occasional lapse into 'broad Yorkshire' that afflicted the good lady when under any emotional strain and correctly interpreted this as a sign of approval.

The housekeeper gave a final sniff and began to clear the table, loading the empty dishes onto a trolley which she whisked away into the kitchen. Some minutes later, further proof of her approval could be heard as the strains of 'Onward Christian Soldiers' floated tunelessly down the hall. The choice of hymn, given their current quest, struck Jamie as singularly inappropriate. Anything less Christian than his acquaintance with Heilyn and his mother was almost impossible to imagine. Jamie wondered whether even the strict Christianity with which he had been raised showed only a facet of the One and supposed that it must. He knew there had been nothing evil in the Presence that had blessed them yesterday. Nor could Heilyn's interference be condemned when it had given such joy, even, thought Jamie appreciatively, if his methods were unorthodox. And Merlin? He didn't merely consort with unnatural beings, he counted them amongst his closest family. Indeed, even his age went against all the accepted laws of nature. Yet Merlin was the wisest and kindest man Jamie had ever known and he marvelled at the narrow intolerance of a society that would condemn him as a pagan or a crank.

"Merlin, if all the religions in the world worship a Supreme Being, why can't we see that the name doesn't matter? Isn't that Being the same whatever name we use?" The question, coming out of the blue, took Merlin by surprise.

"Why yes, lad. There is only One. Let me explain. I heard it told like this one day. Imagine a room full of people, think of all the different characters you would find. Imagine the room is utterly dark so no-one had the least idea of what it was like. If each group had a candle and lit them one at a time, what would they see?" Jamie pictured the room in his mind and saw the scene that his teacher described. "Each single candle would throw a little light on the faces and surroundings of a small group and every person would interpret what he saw in a different way. Nothing would be clear, but the people near the flame would begin to have an idea of where they were.

"As each candle was lit in turn, each small flame would add to the light and illuminate a little more of the room. But not until all the candles were lit would there be enough light to see clearly and even then, there would be many who would look no further than their own small group." Jamie began to see where the tale was leading. "If you take all the faiths of the world as single and separate they are like solitary candles. What they show is true, but only a small and often obscure part of the Truth which is universal. The One, perhaps, is too vast for mortal mind to comprehend in Its entirety, but never make the mistake of scorning the drop because it is not the ocean. Every drop is an essential part of the whole."

Jamie had food enough for thought, so, thanking the old man he went in search of the information Merlin needed, while he, in turn, repaired to delve in his own strange collection of books.

Rhea, alone in the studio, considered the blank canvas. She already had a lot of quick sketches to work from but could not decide where to begin. The events of the past few days were almost incredible, those of the last few hours overwhelming. Unlooked for and unheralded, her heart had been awakened and the past had paled and receded. Not forgotten, no, but faded and distant. Only Anna stood bright and clear against the sepia tints of memory, while Alec was the beacon guiding her toward a future she had not envisioned for herself.

"…When the beast awakes remember that the light will guide the blind through the darkness." The words of Heilyn's message seemed to follow on from her thoughts. She didn't understand it all yet, but Rhea thought that here was a subject that she should try and paint.

She made no sketch, simply allowed the picture to form itself as it would. The brushes moved almost of their own accord, the colours stark against the black canvas she had made.

Time had no meaning for Rhea as she painted, totally absorbed in the act of creation she was unaware of Merlin's entry until he took the brush from her hand and laid it down. She looked around startled, to find that the old man had brought her a tray of sandwiches and fruit.

"Mrs Long insisted that I see you fed and watered, my dear. She was quite concerned that you might miss your lunch."

"I'm sorry, I hadn't realised the time!"

"Oh, it's quarter to twelve, child. In fact, if you don't get a move on you won't have time to change before Alec arrives." Merlin pulled out a chair for Rhea and sat her down. He studied her face and added, "You might want to wash your face too, that shade of yellow does nothing for your nose."

"Oh dear, am I covered in paint again? It seems to go everywhere when I get really involved in a picture."

"No, and you would still look beautiful to Alec, child." Rhea blushed, but Merlin's smile was very warm and gentle. "I know it's none of my business child, nor shall I seek to pry. I shall simply say thank you. There is Light in what you have wrought." He had to clear his throat and began to bustle about, making tea for them both, instructing Rhea to eat and spare him Mrs Long's reproaches.

Two business-like mugs of tea, such as are only found in Yorkshire, were presently deposited on the table and Merlin asked if he might look at Rhea's painting.

"Of course. It isn't finished yet and I'm not sure where it came from. I was thinking about Heilyn's message when I began it."

"So I see. The Light in the darkness." Merlin scrutinised the canvas for several minutes before passing any further comment. Like any painter, Rhea was anxious for a verdict on her work and was glad when Merlin finally spoke. "I think that you have found the key which has eluded me throughout my search today."

The canvas had been given a base coat of black gesso on which the colours sparkled. There was a barren gill with the course of a stream, dry and stony, straddled by a great black dog with eyes of flame. A figure crouched before it in terror, the arms raised to protect itself from the gaping maw of the beast. Yet behind all this was a form of delicate beauty, indistinct in shades of blue and white, like stars on a misty evening.

"What can you see, Merlin?"

"Hope, my child, hope."

Rhea tried to explain this to Alec later that day and asked what he made of it all.

"...and he wouldn't say any more than that?" asked Alec.

"Only that he thought we would be able to work it out for ourselves," Rhea answered, leaning back against him as they sat on the bank of the Wharfe, watching the water as it swirled on its way to the sea, tumbling the stones of the riverbed in its turbulent current. Alec had told her that the river swelled in winter, becoming far deeper and more treacherous than it now appeared on a balmy afternoon.

They had crossed the river by car in Ilkley and walked through Middleton Wood to this spot, talking all the time, beginning to fill the gaps in their knowledge of each other, wanting to share themselves. Rhea had told him a little of her life with Michael, hiding nothing and feeling comfortable enough to speak to Alec of her past. This, she supposed, was truly a measure of trust. She talked of Anna, both as a child and now, as a young woman, lovely and intelligent and with the impulsive streak that had led her into all kinds of adventures.

Alec could hear the love and pride in her voice as she spoke of her daughter and felt a twinge of something akin to jealously, which had not affected him at all when she had spoken of her late husband. He pushed the feeling away. Love could wear many guises and love for her daughter took nothing from what Rhea had given to him. He still felt almost dazed at the fact that she loved him at all!

In his turn, Alec told her of his boyhood, his own adoration of his mother evident in every tale. His father, a successful and presumably busy man, figured little in the narrative, while his sister, Sabrina, had grown from a minor pest to a major problem in her teens, finally beginning to grow up over the last couple of years. Alec spoke of her with the exasperated tolerance he would have shown a naughty kitten.

The air was warm and still under the trees and Rhea, feeling like a teenager and glad she was old enough to appreciate it, slipped off her shoes and dipped her feet into the cold waters of the river. The polished gravel of the riverbed was pleasant underfoot and tucking up her skirt like a schoolgirl, she waded out into the stream, holding out a hand to Alec and laughingly daring him to join her.

Nothing loath, he stripped off his shoes and socks and rolled his trousers up to the knees, wading in to catch her round the waist. He pulled her to him and kissed her long and deeply, the water swirling endlessly around their feet until they both felt they were being swept away by unseen currents.

They felt the water rising around and through them as if they were as insubstantial as the breeze. Alec turned Rhea around to face what he had seen. Standing within the protective circle of his arms, Rhea watched the maelstrom forming around them, whipping the waters to a white foam. A tall figure emerged from the centre of the whirlpool, robed in the shifting blue of reflected skies.

"Champions of Light, I am the guardian of this stream. You stand amid angry waters and face fear with courage. The Horned One gave you the blessing of the Powers of Earth. It falls to me to give the benediction of Water, the blood of Earth." The Lady raised her hands, and from them flowed a shower of rainbows that danced around Alec and Rhea, their touch a zephyr which played though their hair and caressed their lips before returning to the Lady's hand. The two mortals bowed their heads in reverent wonder.

"I have a gifting for you. Where all is barren, remember me. Within my realm I may be summoned at need. Fare well."

The whirling waters receded as Alec called,

Lady, we do not know your name!" But the only reply was the song of the water at their feet.

Elizabeth's greeting, a little while later, told Rhea quite clearly that Alec had already spoken to her on the telephone at some point earlier in the day. She held Rhea in a delicate embrace before leading her to the couch and sitting down beside her, taking one of Rhea's hands in her own.

"Alec," his mother commanded, "run along and help Gwennie in the kitchen, I want to talk to Rhea for a while." She shooed him away with a smile and turned to Rhea. "Don't worry, dear, I'm not going to ask if your intentions are honourable. Not that it's any of my business, but I think a few dishonourable intentions on your part would do him more good!" She laughed at Rhea's surprise. "I may be old, but there is enough of the unregenerate Eve in me still to remember the uncertainties of new love. My dear, you have worked wonders! My sober Alec couldn't wait to tell me about you this morning! He was almost completely unable to finish a sentence and I read far more from the way he spoke than from the few words he managed to string together! I must be a wicked mother, for I thoroughly enjoyed hearing my son reduced to incoherent monosyllables!" A mischievous chuckle accompanied her words and Rhea could not help but smile, any worries about Elizabeth's approval had been quickly dispersed.

"Doesn't it worry you at how quickly this has happened?" Rhea asked. "Something this strong should take a long time to develop."

"You love him so very much?" Rhea took her time to frame her reply, wanting to describe the multi-layered depth of her emotions.

"Yes, I do. From the start, I found him attractive, although his manner was distant and hurtful. He cares about people, but only seems to show it to those who are really close to him. I trust him completely, though I suppose in many ways I barely know him. I think he would be a good friend, the kind who are few and far between; he would do anything for Merlin or Jamie and never count the cost to himself.

"He would be very easy to hurt, I think, his heart runs very deep, doesn't it? Apart from that, we have little in common and we only met a few days ago! Yet, I feel as if I'd spent my life marking time and waiting for him. I love him in so many ways. When I'm with him the world feels exciting, vivid and full of new life, yet I feel safe and comfortable," Rhea's face glowed, "and half the time I feel like a silly teenager, in love for the first time. It is wonderful and a little scary too!"

"Have you told him all this, child?"

"She just did." Alec had been standing unnoticed by the door, aware that he was eavesdropping but unable to resist the chance to find out what Rhea really felt. She had told him in everything but words and he knew, but loving her so much himself he still found it difficult to accept that she could love him in return. He was profoundly grateful for his mother's question and moved by his love's reply.

Elizabeth could sense the almost palpable tension between them and sought for a way to lighten the atmosphere. Assuming a tone of mock severity she chided her son for listening to a conversation which did not concern him at all, apologised to Rhea for his poor upbringing and made her promise to encourage him to mend his manners.

Rhea entered into the spirit of the game and agreed gravely that something would have to be done about him, shaking her head mournfully.

"…and I suppose you didn't even have the courtesy to tell Gwen," was Elizabeth's final shot.

"Lord, no!" was the horrified reply. "She'd have the wedding cake in the oven before supper!" Two pairs of feminine eyes regarded him with pity as Alec realised the implications of the gaffe he'd just made.

The three talked for a little while longer before Alec announced that they would have to leave to meet Jamie and Merlin for the rendezvous in Trollers Gill.

"Take care of each other, my children. My love and my blessing go with you, now and always." Elizabeth hugged them both. "Call me when you get back, no matter what time it is, I will be waiting."

Hand in hand the couple set off on the most dangerous expedition of their lives. Elizabeth watched them go with a fear in her heart she had kept hidden during their visit.

Chapter Ten

TROLLERS GILL

The party left the car near the bridge at Skyreholme Beck and with the setting sun at their backs began the uphill walk to Trollers Gill. The ill equipped expedition at sunset went against all Jamie's warnings about hill walking, but Merlin had assured them that his presence and unique talents would be ample protection against the disasters which normally attended such foolhardiness. The first demonstration of his extraordinary skills came when the mage suggested he should scout ahead and see if he could gain any idea of the location of the trolls' cave before the rest of the party arrived at the gill.

"Do you think it wise to split up?" asked Jamie.

"Oh, I shan't be long, boy," chuckled Merlin. "Just follow the trail till I'm back." The air around them shimmered in the way they had come to recognise when magic was afoot and Merlin was gone. In his place was a ragged-eared owl which regarded them through peat brown eyes. Merlin took a second or two to adjust to the new form, fluttered his feathers and flew off. Where the bird had been was now a glowing orb, about the size of a cricket ball, which bobbed up and down in mid-air as if waiting for them.

"What now?"

"We follow the trail," said Alec, taking Rhea's hand and stepping towards the light. The will o' the wisp advanced, keeping pace with their steps. Jamie shrugged and followed. They continued up the rock strewn slopes for about ten minutes before hearing a low hoot, heralding Merlin's return. There was too little light now to see when the air coalesced into the mage's form and the orb extinguished itself.

"Well, I know the location of the cave. There seem to be two trolls living in the cliff to the right hand side of the vale, where it narrows significantly towards Gill Heads, the old waterfall which closes the end of the trail. The only way through there is up. We could have bypassed the Gill and gone around, but then we wouldn't be where we are supposed to be." Merlin brushed himself down and gave himself a small shake, trying to fit back into human shape after the freedom of the avian form. "I don't want to be occupied with the trolls till the last minute, for once I turn my attention to them I will be unable to help you much. Jamie, you will have to watch the trolls and gauge their reaction to my illusion," he continued. "I'm relying on you to keep an eye on Alec and Rhea too. You will have to judge where the peril is greatest and call me if I am needed more with them than with the trolls.

"Alec and Rhea, you must try and work your way up the gill towards its end. I don't know what will happen, but I believe you have been given certain clues and will be able to answer any danger between you. Remember all the tales and legends you know about the area, Alec. The clues are there, I'm sure. I wish I had something more concrete to go on."

"Stop worrying, old man," came a mocking voice.

"Heilyn!"

"I'm only here for moral support, before you ask!" said the newcomer, throwing up his hands. "I thought you might like to be reassured. You *do* have all the clues, you know. I'm not allowed to say more than that. These two," nodding at Alec and Rhea, "were given a gift this afternoon.

How's your Latin, Alec?" The tone was light and conversational, but Alec's frown deepened as he tried to fathom the further clue he felt sure he had just been given.

"Is there nothing you can add, Heilyn?" Rhea asked. Heilyn shook his head in regret.

"Only my blessing to add to those you have already received." He stared hard at Alec as if trying to communicate something. Merlin, for once neither annoyed nor contemptuous, bowed gravely to his half-brother.

"I alone of this company can appreciate what you have already given, brother."

"May the Light guide your steps tonight." The reply was sober as the figure vanished in the darkness.

"What was he trying to tell us, Merlin?"

"I'm not sure, Jamie. I'm working on it. Shall we go on?"

Very soon, it seemed to Rhea, they reached the entrance to the gill. Tall limestone cliffs bounded the vale on two sides, the end of the valley was already lost in the night. Suddenly, at the limit of their field of vision, a dark shape crashed to the rocky floor.

"They can smell us," said Merlin. "From here we must advance carefully. Good luck and may the Light guide us all."

Slowly they moved deeper between the cliffs as the boulders rained down ahead of them, the noise alone terrifying. One great rocked shattered only feet in front of them and Merlin stopped.

"I must deal with them now. Use the light I create to judge when it is safe to go on. Jamie, you must be my eyes." He smiled at them in loving encouragement, then turned to face the cliff, head bowed, with an expression of total concentration on his face, shutting out the world around him, his will focussed on his task.

Jamie hugged Rhea and Alec and took up his place at the old man's side. Alec tightened his grip on Rhea's hand and drew her close to await the opportunity Merlin was attempting to provide.

For several minutes nothing seemed to happen to stop the crushing boulders raining down around them. Alec thought it little short of miraculous that they had not already been hit. Gradually, the sky above the waterfall began to lighten, becoming suffused with the pink and gold of a summer dawn. In the growing light, their aggressors became visible. Rhea was glad they had not been able to see them before.

Giants, they were, appearing to stand seven feet tall on the slope above them, gnarled and weathered as the rocks they hurled at the trespassers, with jagged teeth reaching below their bottom jaws. Vaguely humanoid in shape they yet lacked any semblance of kinship with the race of men and their howls of lust and rage as they saw the company below them were unlike anything Rhea had ever heard. To her petrified imagination they sounded like the splitting of rocks deep beneath the earth's crust, granite shrieking under earthquake pressure.

Rocks pounded around the party. Alec pulled Rhea this way and that, trying to shield her with his own body from the flying limestone. One great slab crashed on the rocks beside them, sending up showers of sharp splinters. Alec, oblivious to the blood trickling down his cheek, heard Rhea cry out and saw a dark stain spreading down her sleeve. Cursing, he pulled a handkerchief from his pocket and tied it roughly around the shredded sleeve, unable to do more under the rain of stones. The howls from above held a triumphant note as the smell of blood reached the trolls.

The sky continued to brighten, casting a soft illumination over the valley. The trolls were watching the false dawn, attention divided between the light and their prey. Jamie had been sure they were going to charge down the cliff and had his hand poised ready to rouse Merlin from the trance-like state. The trolls were glancing more and more towards the east, then with a scream of frustration they turned and scrambled back toward the cave mouth, which shimmered and closed behind them as if it had never been.

"Merlin! It's alright, they've gone!" Jamie touched the mage on the sleeve, but he shook his head and replied through gritted teeth,

"It's an illusion; as soon as I let it go they'll be back. Go, Rhea, go!"

Rhea and Alec stumbled forward hand in hand, conscious of danger and unaware of what exactly they were supposed to do. Walking blindly to face unknown peril in pursuit of a mysterious goal was perhaps the most terrifying thing they could have been asked to attempt.

They followed the course of the dry stream bed, walking east towards Gill Heads and Merlin's dawn, picking their way carefully over the rocks in the soft light, driven by a sense of urgency. Strain was showing in the stiff limbs and the terror was mounting as they stumbled on. A feeling of being watched made Rhea continually glance up at the hidden cave, the back of her neck tingled unpleasantly and she was glad of Alec's grip on her hand.

Without warning a great black shape rose from the rocks in front of them, head down and snarling. Jamie, watching from the distance, caught his breath. The dog-like creature was as big as a bear, heavy with malice and hunger. Large, round eyes burned with cold flame and yellow fangs gleamed against the red maw of the Barguest.

The creature stood astride the dry stream bed, just below the invisible entrance to the trolls cave. Jamie dare not disturb the mage for fear of releasing the trolls, yet dare not leave his friends to face the beast unaided.

"Alec, Rhea, its eyes! Don't look in its eyes!" Alec spun Rhea around to face him, glancing at Jamie in comprehension and rapidly using Rhea's silk scarf to blindfold her. The young man watched as his friend stooped and grabbed a handful of stones. He began to edge around the Barguest, dragging Rhea behind him and brandishing the paltry weapon. The creature gathered itself to pounce and Alec hurled the first rock. It hit the beast square on the head and the Barguest yelped, backing off a pace.

Jamie's mind raced as he tried to think of some way to help. Eyes. Running water. Death. There was something Rhea had said. A gift. Called at need. Who? Who was the Lady from the river? The stream used to flow down the gill to join the Wharfe below. There was a Roman altar in the churchyard in Ilkley dedicated to the river goddess....

Alec threw another rock but the beast ignored it, snarling and continued its advance. Jamie saw the dog lunge and Rhea fell at its feet, in seconds she would be beyond help. Alec hurled himself at the monster, grabbing its ear and twisting, pounding with fists and feet.

"Rhea! Call on the Lady!" Jamie screamed, hoping she would understand. "Call Verbeia! She is the guardian!"

The snarling dog tore at Alec, worrying him like a toy. Jamie saw Rhea struggle to her feet, arms raised. She called a name and the ring on her right hand glowed with a clear blue light which was answered by the flash of lightning from above Gill Heads.

There was a sound of splintering stone and the thunder of water rushing down the long-dry channel from the waterfall. The great beast lifted its head and howled, the sound echoing off the cliffs in a crescendo of despair as the water gushed around its feet. As Jamie watched, the Barguest thrashed and struggled in the shallow water, seeming to shrivel and implode, leaving behind only the stench of decay.

Jamie could no longer stand and watch. He pelted over to where Rhea, the blindfold torn from her eyes, was hauling the wounded man from the water and helped her to drag him to the relative safety of the bank. Alec was limp and unconscious, bleeding profusely from innumerable gashes on his shoulders and arms.

"Take care of him, Jamie," she implored. "I must go on." She kissed Alec once on the lips, then without a backward glance, she set off alone, head high and straight backed, a valiant figure alone in the pale light.

Rhea dare not look back for fear that her courage would desert her. Leaving Alec in that state was breaking her heart, but she knew, somehow, what she had to do and only success would give meaning to Alec's suffering.

Her feet seemed to know the way and she let them carry her towards her goal. At the end of the vale was now a crashing waterfall which barred her path, but above it was a silvery blue flame which somehow she needed to reach.

Ignoring the pain in her arm and the ache in her heart, she began the dangerous ascent, clutching at rocks invisible beneath the tumbling waters. The force of the torrent battered her already aching body and threatened to throw her back. Water invaded her mouth and eyes, blinding her and making breathing almost impossible, but she persevered with grim determination. Her feet slid on the wet stone and rocks came away in hands so cold they could barely grasp. Her chest was on fire and her wet clothes dragged her down.

Rhea never knew how she accomplished that perilous climb. Drenched and exhausted, she fell face down on a rock and lay gasping for breath, unaware of the compassionate gaze of the lady in blue.

"Heart of Earth, you are safe now." The voice was gentle and not unfamiliar. Rhea forced herself to her knees and found herself before the lady from the river, the argent light surrounding her as she stood amid the waters of her new-born cascade.

"Verbeia?" One word was all she could manage.

"That was the name they gave me," she conceded. "There were others. I am glad that you found a name by which to summon me. Long has this vale lain barren beneath the feet of the Barguest. Your call, here at the limit of my domain, has permitted me to act at last to cleanse and renew the source of my stream. You have earned gratitude this night." Rhea fought her weariness and pulled herself to her feet.

"Thank you, lady, for saving us from the Barguest. If gratitude is due then it is you who have earned it." The lady shook her head in denial.

"You must go on, to the Mouth of Hell, to claim what you came here to seek. Have faith, daughter and do not falter. Fear is the only enemy left to conquer this night. Go with the blessing of Verbeia upon you." Rhea found herself enveloped in the silver glow of the evanescent figure. She bowed her head in respect and when she raised it again she was alone.

Rhea clambered to the bank and followed the course of the swirling stream, taking great care in the false light. She was anxious to complete her task and return to Alec, but heeded the warnings and took care to pick a safe route among the stones.

She had lost track of time long ago and had no idea how long it took her to reach a place where a gaping chasm blocked her way. This, she guessed from the cursory look she had given the map, must be Hell Hole. She sank to her knees on the crumbling edge and peered down into blackness. There was no way down. She leaned over, ever more precariously, not knowing what she was supposed to do.

What she saw took her breath away. Suspended in mid-air, some twenty feet below, gleamed a bright metal object, long and slender. Her eyes scanned the ground and the sides of the hole to find a way down. She found none. The sword hung impossibly in the air. Far from the chasm walls, too high to reach from the bottom, too low to reach from the edge.

Rhea knelt back from the deadly drop to consider the problem. She had no rope and nothing with which to improvise. Only one improbable idea came to mind. Leaning back out over the edge, she stretched out her hand and called to the blade with all the force of her will. Slowly, almost imperceptibly, the sword began to rise. With renewed confidence Rhea bent her whole being to calling the sword to her hand and, slowly, incredibly, it came.

After five minutes Rhea was drenched in perspiration, but the shining blade was only inches from her grasp. She reached out, sending a shower of stones tumbling into the depths, and grasped the hilt. At last, clutching her prize to her breast, she retreated to a safe distance to get her pounding heart under control. Somewhere a bird began to sing, heralding the true dawn.

Rhea was amazed at the time that had passed. The sword was heavy, perhaps half as tall as she. The blade was made of a bright, white metal, with a woven pattern where the steel had been folded by the smith. The hilt was black, fashioned of some substance Rhea could not identify, inlaid with an equilateral triangle, the point facing down the blade and crossed by a curious wave. Cradling the sword in her arms she made her way to the head of the cascade and looked down.

Merlin had abandoned his vigil and knelt with Jamie beside the supine form of Alec, who was moving, trying to sit up, it seemed, in spite of protests from his friends. Rhea held the sword aloft and the first rays of the sun caught the blade, turning it into a shaft of purest light.

The three below saw the flash and turned as one in the direction of the falls. Jamie punched the air in sheer delight. Merlin stood proud to greet her and Alec, untended for the moment, struggled upright. Coursing unheeded down his cheeks the salt tears stung his wounds, the pain ignored in the flood of relief as he recognised the shining figure above the falls.

"Jamie, take Alec down to the stile. I'll meet you there." The air rippled and Merlin once more changed shape and a glorious falcon took to the air, winging its way in joyful flight to where Rhea waited.

Rhea ached in every muscle. Her hands, she noted with surprise, were raw and bleeding sluggishly from the climb and she was shivering with cold. The gash on her arm throbbed horribly, but she was so wet she could not tell if it was bleeding.

Merlin, assuming his own form once more, threw his coat around her shoulders. He was humbled by the courage she had shown, armed with nothing more than her own humanity, in the face of such extraordinary foes.

Rhea leaned on the sword, in the battle weary posture of the warrior, only pride keeping her on her feet. It seemed fitting when the ancient mage bent his knee before her.

"I said that I had chosen well, Swordbearer."

Jamie and Alec were sitting by the stile when Merlin and Rhea came into view. She was leaning heavily on the old man, exhaustion showing in every line of her body, yet a strange inner glow lit her face. The two men pulled themselves to their feet as Rhea approached, Jamie leaping the stile to go lend a hand. He stopped, staring in awe at the heavy blade that Rhea cradled in her arms like a babe, the reality of the night's adventure hitting him with all the force of a brick.

Rhea handed the sword to Merlin and hugged the boy fiercely. Without his quick thinking, she dared not consider what might have happened. The she turned to Alec, who waited still, covering the distance between them without releasing him from her searching gaze.

She almost fell into his arms, the last of her strength ebbing away as he held her to him, her head against his throat, holding each other close, the pain of their injuries almost welcome as proof of each other's nearness. Merlin looked on, beaming, the sight almost as valuable to him as the sword he now held.

It took a while to get back to the car. All four were feeling the effects of the night and neither Rhea nor Alec was in a fit state to move quickly. As soon as they were installed in the vehicle, Jamie turned the car for home and Alec tapped out Elizabeth's number on the mobile phone.

"Mother? Yes, all safe. A few cuts and bruises, we'll soon mend. Merlin convinced the trolls it was dawn sometime before midnight and Jamie, God bless him, saved us from the Barguest." He listened to a barrage of questions until Merlin reached back and took the phone from his hands.

"Elizabeth, dear… Merlin. Listen, I'm going to put the children to bed then I'll come over and give you an update. About eleven? Very well, I'll see you then. Yes. I'll tell them." He switched the phone off completely before handing it back to Alec with instructions to leave it that way. "She sends you all her love and said to tell you she is proud of you all. So am I. You were tested to the limits back there and showed your true colours. Do not belittle what you each have achieved, even in your own minds!"

"Fear blinded us to the hope in Verbeia's gift," said Rhea. "It was Jamie who gave us light to see by."

"No, my dear," replied the mage, "it was friendship, trust and love for each other that gave light to us all." He glanced at Jamie, whose face broke into the now familiar grin as the old man added, "Even Heilyn has his uses!"

By the time they arrived back at Stone Lodge, Alec and Rhea were asleep on the back seat of the car. Merlin woke Rhea and instructed her to get a shower before coming up to the house for breakfast.

"If we can get organised before Mrs Long gets here, it will make my life a lot easier!" he explained. "Alec can have a bath at the house and Jamie can lend him some clean clothes." Jamie laughed and pointed out that Alec was both taller and broader than he. "Don't worry; I'll do any alterations we need." Somehow Jamie did not think the old man was planning on using a needle and thread.

"What about the sword?" asked Rhea.

"Up to you, my dear. Take it with you, or leave it with me while you rest."

"Keep it for me, Merlin, until I feel more like myself. In fact, I think you should take it with you when you go to see Elizabeth. She must have suffered as much as any of us last night, not knowing what was happening. She deserves the chance to see it too."

"Thank you, Rhea, I think she would feel honoured. Now go and get cleaned up or we'll have a lot of explaining to do before breakfast!"

Rhea let herself into the cottage and decided that a bath would be of more use to her stiff and aching muscles than a shower. She was vaguely surprised that her teeth had stopped chattering and she didn't feel completely frozen. She supposed that having a mage in their party had its advantages, and smiled as she stripped off her filthy clothes and threw them in the washing machine. She lowered herself gingerly into the steaming tub and gave herself up to the heat for a while.

Only the stinging of the cuts on her hands and the throbbing of her arm kept her awake. She cleaned her hands carefully, removing the grit from the abrasions. Her arm was an altogether different matter. She kept it out of the water lest the heat make it start bleeding again. She hadn't removed the makeshift bandage which Alec had tied around her arm through the lacerated sleeve and did not want to disturb the wound till she was clean. Washing her hair was awkward one handed and she was thankful her short crop of curls would require no more than brushing to look tidy.

Rhea checked the time. Breakfast wouldn't be long and tired as she was, she knew that food would do her good. Struggling, she removed the handkerchief from her arm. If there was a first aid kit in the cottage, she had not found it, and was obliged to improvise, using two of Mrs Long's pristine linen napkins. One she folded into a pad and laid over the ragged gash while the other served as a bandage to hold it in place. To avoid that good lady's curiosity she added a long sleeved shirt in navy blue over the white vest and jeans. Satisfied that she looked presentable, Rhea made her way to rejoin the others.

Jamie was alone in the dining room, looking no worse for the adventures of the previous night. Rhea envied him the stamina of youth. He pulled out a chair for her and handed her a cup of strong, sweet tea. Rhea, who took her tea unsweetened, grimaced at the taste, but drank it when she was told to.

"It will do you good and Merlin told me to see you had it. He won't be long. He's looking after Alec."

"How is he?" asked Rhea.

"Exhausted, my dear." The reply came from Merlin, who closed the door behind him. "I have put him to bed in the spare room and tended to his cuts and scratches. He was in a rather bad way, but I know a trick or two that are not in the medical books. He'll do, though he'll be a little sore for a few days."

While he spoke, Merlin had been filling a plate with scrambled eggs, bacon and tomatoes, which he deposited in front of Rhea with an injunction to eat, while Jamie began to tell them of the night's adventure from his perspective.

Rhea was certain she could not possibly eat a cooked breakfast and was considerably surprised a few minutes later to realise that she had. Not only did she clear the portion Merlin had served her, but also several pieces of toast and marmalade that Jamie had prepared for her and placed at her elbow, along with two more cups of the syrup-like tea.

Judging by the smug expressions of the two gentlemen seated opposite her, she realised that she had been outmanoeuvred, but had to admit that she felt much better for the substantial meal.

"If you have quite finished eating, Rhea, shall we escape to the library before the sergeant major comes in to clear up?" Jamie asked, a picture of innocence. Rhea laughed and rose, preceding the men from the room. "We'll smuggle you out before she sees you, then you can get some sleep."

"May I look in on Alec first?"

"Of course, child," answered Merlin. "He looks rather bruised, I'm afraid, but I promise you, if he sleeps for a few hours he will look a lot better."

"I shan't wake him," she replied.

"No, you won't," chuckled Merlin. "He refuses to go to sleep until he has seen you safe. He made me promise to feed you first though. This way."

He led Rhea along the narrow passage to its end, where he opened a door and stepped aside, waiting for her to enter.

Alec was rather pale against the white sheets and Rhea was glad of Merlin's assurances. He had a nasty cut on the temple and what looked to be teeth marks on his arms and shoulders. He opened his eyes as Rhea entered and smiled.

"How are you feeling, Alec?"

"Like a rag doll," he grinned, "How about you?"

"A little sore, but I'll be fine when I'm rested. I've certainly been well fed!" Rhea glared in mock annoyance at Merlin, who stood by the door and smiled like an elderly cherub. "Merlin said you need to sleep, so I shan't stay." She leaned down and kissed him lightly, wincing a little at the pain in her arm as she supported herself.

"How's the arm?" asked Alec.

"What's this? What is wrong with your arm, Rhea?" Merlin demanded. Alec looked at her in reproach.

"Why have you not mentioned it to Merlin?"

"It's okay now. I dressed it earlier," dismissed Rhea. But Merlin was having none of it. Alec described what had happened and Rhea was made to sit on the bed and remove her shirt. Merlin carefully peeled back the napkins and Rhea was obliged to endure a lecture on the folly of trying to deal with the wound herself.

Dried blood had firmly glued the second napkin to the wound and when it was removed the exposed gash oozed red. Jamie was sent in search of the first aid kit and hot water, while Rhea endured the thorough examination of the wound.

"It is clean enough, but the flesh is jaggedly torn. It ought to be stitched, but I think I can at least spare you that!" Merlin cleaned the cut, Jamie holding the bowl of water and Alec squeezing Rhea's hand for comfort. A small pot of something smelling not unpleasantly of flowers was opened and the contents liberally applied.

"Agrimony and marigold ointment, I've used it for years," Merlin volunteered, "and pass that jar labelled 'arnica' please, Jamie. It will help the bruising on her back." Merlin applied the ointment to her hands and arm before liberally swabbing her bruised back with the lotion. He kept up a running commentary as he worked, telling them of the different herbs and their curative properties.

"It is good to see the old remedies coming back again, but without all the mumbo-jumbo that used to be associated with folk medicine. So many modern drugs are based on plant extracts, natural or synthesised, yet science has ridiculed the herbalist for a century or more. There is a great deal of satisfaction in being proved right." He stepped back to survey his handiwork. "Yes, that will do nicely. Now, if you could all keep quiet for a moment, I'll attend to the 'stitches'."

Merlin laid his fingertips lightly on Rhea's arm, pushing the ragged edges of the wound into place. Minute tongues of white fire danced over Rhea's skin and she watched, barely surprised, as the torn flesh began to hold together. The process took just a few minutes and yet the arm looked as if it had been healing for a week or more. The inflammation had gone and the wound had settled. Rhea felt exhausted and even Merlin looked a little grey. Rhea thanked him warmly as she replaced her shirt.

"It will ache, of course, and be stiff for a while. What you need now is sleep." Merlin shot a concerned glance at Alec. "You too! Off with you, young woman. You can come back this afternoon, but not before tea, mind!" Rhea dropped a kiss on Alec's brow and another on the wrinkled cheek of the old man and Alec was left to sleep at last.

Rhea fell fully clothed on the bed in the cottage, pulling the eiderdown over her feet and was herself asleep in no time at all.

Jamie and Merlin meanwhile, had ensconced themselves in the library. Merlin wanted the younger man to get some sleep, but was obliged to concede that Jamie did indeed seem wide awake and full of energy.

"Would you care to come with me to visit Elizabeth?"

"If you don't need me, I think I'd like to go for a walk," replied Jamie. "Some fresh air will do me good." Merlin regarded him quizzically.

"You didn't get enough fresh air last night?" Jamie looked rather uncomfortable and Merlin waited for the rest of the tale.

"To tell you the truth, things have been moving so fast I just feel the need to get up on the moor alone for a while. Think things through, you know." He stood, and took to pacing the floor, hands thrust deep in his pockets. "Until last night, it all seemed fairly straightforward. You know. Defeat monsters, find magic sword, save the world, then go home for tea." He stopped pacing and looked Merlin straight in the eye. "Oh, part of me understood the importance of what we are trying to do here, but it all so far outside my frame of reference that it hadn't really registered. People got hurt out there last night, Merlin. My friends!"

"Sit down, Jamie, and I shall try to help." The Keeper of Light silently invoked his Masters and asked for their guidance.

He took the sword from its resting place on the great oak desk, and laid it across Jamie's hands. The young man felt a thrill as the cold metal touched his outstretched palms, he was holding far more than an ancient blade. He could feel the weight of years and the depth of power pulsing through his fingers and coursing around his body. It was not the voice of his friend who continued, but the voice of the Keeper, resonant with ageless hope.

"There is a price to pay for power, always. This the Oldest Ones knew at the dawn of our age of the world when they offered up their bloody sacrifices. In their eyes it was not murder, but a gift to the gods. They had little and chose to give the one precious thing, Jamie: life. The victims, if such we may call them, were honoured to be chosen and were, in their faith, guaranteed a place with the gods in the afterlife. Thus, they often went willing to their death.

"One thing the Old Ones did not understand, however. It is not the death that buys power but the faith of the willing sacrifice. They knew enough to believe it to be a bad omen for the chosen one to resist death and often prevented the victim from panicking by the use of drugs. The blood that was spilled by our friends last night was freely given. They knew what they were attempting and what the cost of failure might be. For their faith in our quest and their love for each other they willingly risked all that they are. It is never the blood which buys power, no, but in this case, the blood was the visible symbol of their commitment and voluntary self-sacrifice.

"Nor need blood always be the appointed symbol; sometimes the sacrifice made is internal and known only to the gods and the one who offers it. Only the spirit in which the offering is made has any value, and true sacrifice is always answered. Do you understand, my boy?"

"I think so, Merlin. I know Alec waded into the Barguest last night with no hesitation when Rhea was threatened. I think he would have traded his life for hers last night without question."

"That, Jamie, is another misapprehension shared by many. You may not bargain with the gods. Remember that they are even more deeply bound to natural law than we, being, you might say, created to epitomise that law. You cannot say 'I will give you this in return for that', only the first three words hold any value."

"'I will give...' yes, I see."

"I hope so, Jamie. It is not an easy lesson to learn in a world that glorifies wealth and possessions. We learn to take before we can walk, redressing that balance is a difficult task which we all face and many never achieve."

The old man took the sword from his hands as he spoke and laid it back on the desk.

"Go for your walk, my boy. Let the wind blow some clean air into your brain, it must be reeling from all it has had to cope with in the last few days. Make sure to take the mobile with you for safety's sake and don't stay out too long." The old man's smile was as warm as the summer sun. "I must go and tell Beth a story."

Chapter Eleven

CLOSE ENCOUNTER

Jamie had set out with no clear destination in mind, following the same path he had taken just days before with Rhea. It was one of those bright and windy days beloved of walkers, yet being mid-week there was no-one to be seen any closer than the Cow and Calf. The Yorkshire Dales known by tourists didn't seem to extend this close to Leeds and Bradford, for which Jamie was thankful, although Rombald's Moor was the barrier between Airedale and Wharfedale.

Most of the visitors were locals who looked on the moor as part of their back garden and could be extremely defensive of 'their' property. Jamie recalled with satisfaction the stories of public outcry some years earlier, when plans for a road which would have passed by the stone circle had been broached. The route had been cleared and marked right across the moor, like 'a gurt, 'ungry worm' as John Spencer, a regular at the Malt Shovel had described it. The scar of the road was barely visible now; the moor had closed around it and given it life again.

Jamie followed the course of Coldstone Beck to its source below the Twelve Apostles, one of the other stone circles on the moor. He considered the stones in a new way, feeling more respect than ever before for the builders of this ancient temple.

There was nothing grandiose about the ring of stones, yet this was a holy place and those who had carried the boulders to this high and desolate spot had been far closer to the gods and the land than those who occasionally passed today.

Not far from here was Ashlar Chair, a high rock that looked across the Dale to Simon's Seat. Jamie wondered if the two were connected. The entire moor was dotted, in fact, with ancient sites of forgotten sanctity. Perhaps those who slept beneath the barrows here would have known the answers.

Jamie turned aside from the ascent and strode across the heather in the direction of the long barrow. He was astonished to see that a low doorway had been cut into the side of the mound and guessed that the archaeologists from the dig had been working here. He had met one or two of them at the Malt Shovel and wondered if he could trade on that meagre acquaintance or his position with 'Professor Ambrose' to gain admittance. Jamie grinned at the memory of John Spencer's pungent denunciation of "t' muck grubbers as leaves nowt be". Despite his own interest in local history Jamie had reservations about despoiling the houses of the dead.

There was no-one in sight and no vehicle could have made the ascent to disclose the presence of the archaeologists, nor did anyone appear when he shouted down the tunnel in the barrow. The passage had been carefully made and was rock lined, the floor swept clean. There were no fences or signs to warn of danger so Jamie concluded that there was nothing inside that the team had thought worthy of protection. This being the case, the young man saw no reason not to enter the tomb. He bowed his head in silent apology to the ancient dead who had been entombed here for eternity, only to be dug up by their fellow man, and went inside.

The ceiling was just high enough to walk erect and sufficient light filtered through the doorway to allow him to see for a few yards, after which, Jamie was obliged to fall back on his torch, thankful that it was part of his walking equipment. Rain and fog fall heavy and with little warning on the high moors, blotting out the sun; a torch for bad weather or delay was essential. There were many dangers one did not wish to find by accident in the Dales.

The passage seemed to trace a spiral path into the tumulus, going in a clockwise direction towards the centre, 'deosil' thought Jamie, as opposed to widdershins, anti-clockwise, against the movement of the sun. It was a symbol of life in the house of death. It was an unusual design for a barrow, where there would normally be a short, straight passageway to its heart.

Jamie advanced cautiously, amazed that such extensive excavations had passed unnoticed and wary of where he placed his feet. A gentle light began to glow ahead of him, growing in brightness as he approached and he wondered if the darkness had misled him and he had gone full circle. But the doorway through which he passed out into sunlight was not the same one through which he had entered.

Jamie looked around him in astonishment. He found himself in a clearing surrounded by great oaks bedecked with mistletoe and songbirds. The light was green-gold, filtering through a canopy of leaves which obscured the sky. In the centre of the glade was a small pool of clear water fed by a bubbling spring that rose from the ground at the base of a lone standing stone. The air was very warm and humid and Jamie was thirsty, but under the circumstances he felt obliged to eye the pool with some suspicion. He dipped his hand in the water rather gingerly. Nothing happened. The water was cold and clean, he could see the sandy bottom, free of debris and algae.

"You may drink from my fountain if you thirst." The mellifluous voice made him start and turn, suddenly struck by the strangeness of his situation. Mab was leaning against a tree, the glorious curtain of her hair spreading like a silken stole around her shoulders. She laughed gently at his surprise. "Drink, Jamie, there is no harm here."

Jamie cupped his hands and drank from the pristine waters. Mab knelt beside him and he offered his hands to be a cup for her also. The gown she wore was simple, white with a girdle of silver, and she wore no other adornment save a pair of tiny silver earrings fashioned in the shape of flowers that chimed merrily as she moved. She seemed far removed from the seductress who had fascinated Jamie in Merlin's room. She laughed as if reading his thought.

"That is a game that Merlin and I have been playing for many of your years, but come, sit with me in my forest and we shall speak of your quest."

"Do you think I ought to discuss it with you?"

"Of course!" Mab drew him down on the velvet moss to sit beside her. "I already know all that has passed, silly boy. The Sword of Earth has been granted to the woman, she and the Windlord paid a price for it. Merlin is boasting to Elizabeth and has put the other two to sleep until his return." She counted these points on her long white fingers and smiled at Jamie's expression of surprise. "These things are my concern also, Water Bearer." She studied his face, a smile quivering on the corners of the rosy lips. "I see, it is not my knowledge of these high matters that surprises you. What then?"

"Merlin has 'put' them to sleep?"

"Of course! They could hardly be trusted to stay in separate rooms otherwise, now could they?" She peeped at his through her lashes, "That piece of meddling worked out very well, don't you think?"

Jamie grinned for reply.

"Do you do that kind of thing often?"

"Meddle? Only when it serves a purpose."

"What is your purpose with me?" Jamie asked. Mab stroked his cheek and snared his eyes with hers.

"Whatever you wish…"

What followed in the timeless grove was an experience unlike anything Jamie, in his young life, could ever have imagined. There was a dreamlike quality that made Jamie doubt, later, that his memory of that mating was true. She was everything a woman could be to a man, tender, almost reticent, at one moment, virginal and hesitant another, then finally she was a great crescendo of passion which engulfed and consumed him, obliterating any trace of his own personality.

Quiet, unseen, a shape began to form within the waters of the spring, made from the swirling eddies of the cascade and the dance of light through oak leaves reflected in the silver pool. As Jamie drowned in the act of creation, unknown and unknowing, a being came into existence, born of Water and Light and need.

He awoke as the sun was dropping behind the hills. He rubbed his eyes, disoriented and confused. He must have been more tired than he had realised to fall asleep on the moor. He looked around to get his bearings and realised that he was beside the long barrow. There was no trace of a doorway cut in the side. In spite of the fading light, he walked all the way around the mound to check, but no, he must have dreamed it.

He started back down the moor, wanting to get home before he was missed at dinner, moving as quickly as the poor light allowed over the trackless heather and bilberry carpet. Cursing himself for a careless fool he opted for the quickest route down from the moor, which would take him to the road before the light faded too much, scrambling down Green Crag Slack.

The path he had chosen was rocky and the remains of last year's bracken made the ground slippery underfoot. His torch was no use when he tried it, the batteries were completely dead and he concluded that he must have switched it on accidentally in his pocket.

He made it just in time to meet Merlin as he pulled into the yard.

"Have a good walk?" asked the old man, leaning into the car to collect the cloth wrapped sword.

"Sort of. I went up by the Twelve Apostles then fell asleep near the barrow."

"That seems very unlike you, my boy. Last night must have caught up with you after all." The two shed their coats in the hall and Jamie followed Merlin into the library. "Be a good lad and see if you can't persuade Mrs Long that dinner won't spoil if she holds it back half an hour. You wheedle far better than I and I still have to wake Rhea and Alec." Jamie's brows knit in consternation and Merlin, surprised, asked what was wrong.

"Merlin, did you put them to sleep? By magic, I mean?"
"Yes, my boy, I didn't trust them to stay where they were and rest, so I interfered a little, you might say. Why?" But Jamie just shook his head dismissively and went to cajole the long-suffering housekeeper.

Merlin bent to retrieve something that the young man had dropped. He found himself holding an oak leaf in his hand, yet no oak grew on that part of the moor, he knew.

"Mab?" He was answered only by a whisper on the evening breeze.

"It was needful."

Merlin thoughtfully carried the leaf to the fireplace and cast it into the flames where it blazed green-gold and was consumed.

Rhea awoke next morning feeling much refreshed. Flexing her arm experimentally, she was pleased to discover that the pain had subsided to a dull ache, the bruises had faded overnight to sulphur yellow and most of the soreness had vanished from her abused limbs. She hoped Alec had fared as well and silently blessed Merlin's herb lore.

Dinner had been a quiet meal, only Merlin having much to say. He brought messages of loving support from Elizabeth and kept up a light flow of conversation, telling of her delight and astonishment at their adventure. Rhea and Alec had then been sent back to bed, liberally anointed with Merlin's potions, with instructions to sleep late next morning.

The clock showed Rhea that she, at least, had obeyed this injunction as it was now twenty past eleven. Rising reluctantly, she wandered into the kitchen to make coffee. Waiting for the kettle to boil she contemplated the scene through the window. The sky was heavy with great, dark clouds and the moor was shrouded in mist. It must have been raining heavily as the stones of the wall were dripping and the grass below trembled under the weight of the droplets they had caught.

She carried her coffee through into the living room and collected her mail from the mat. No letter from Anna, two lurid envelopes offering 'unmissable' deals and a folded note. The shocking pink and lime envelopes were consigned to the wastepaper basket on the general principle that anything that needed to be that colour was best left unopened. The note she carried back to the sofa where she curled up with her coffee to read it.

Love,

I hope you are quite well today. Merlin's weeds have worked marvels for me! I expected to be out of action for some time, but I feel ready for anything this morning! I have gone back to Ivy Place to bathe and change into some of my own clothes. Jamie is not happy with Merlin's efforts as a tailor and swears I have stretched his jumpers out of all recognition! Given their usual shape, I wouldn't have thought he'd have noticed!

I didn't want to disturb you this morning in case you were still sleeping. Merlin and Jamie have both gone off somewhere and are being singularly uncommunicative about their destination. I don't think they had planned anything till Merlin had a phone call. No doubt we will be told when they get back. They said they'd be back for teatime and I'll be back around four too. Don't go out on the moor, the rain will have made it very boggy. Stay indoors and rest, love. I want you healed and whole.

Do you know that I love you very much?

Alec

Rhea read the note twice. Once to read what he had written and once for pure joy. She had no need to rush, so she lingered over her coffee and wallowed in a steamy bath, fragrant with the lavender and comfrey oil Merlin had instructed her to use. By the time she had dressed in a soft lamb's wool tunic and wide skirt, the rain was drumming on the windows again. There seemed little point in getting wet through, so she unpacked her watercolours and sat down to paint at the dining table.

The skies that flowed from the sable brush were as heavy as the ones outside her window, great swathes and wreaths of blue-grey which swallowed the summit of the mountain she painted, rolling down the hillsides to the valley, cutting off the heights so that they seemed to float free of the land to which they belonged. The rain leached all detail and colour from the landscape and she painted in soft blues and misty greys, the one trace of colour a shaft of pale gold light which pierced the cloud cover to strike the top of the hill. The loose style and hazy hues had a quality which reminded Rhea that Turner had loved painting in the Dales.

The rain was hammering at the windows and Rhea did not hear the knock at the door. It was not until the letterbox was rattled that she realised anyone was there. She sprang up to open the door to find Alec dripping on the mat.

"Goodness, you're soaked! Come in and take your coat off." Rhea drew him inside and helped him out of his wet jacket. "Does no-one in Yorkshire use an umbrella?"

"Very rarely," Alec laughed, "we're a hardy lot." As proof of this he took her in his arms and showed her that he had come to no harm from his dousing. "I have missed you, love," he said when they were finally obliged to surface for air. "How are you? Let me see."

Alec held her at arm's length and studied her face, and then he gently rolled up the sleeve which covered the injured arm.

"Whatever is in Merlin's bottles could make him a fortune." Rhea, in turn, subjected him to careful scrutiny and decided that he too, had benefited from Merlin's skill. "I have been up to the Lodge already. Mrs Long says we are to come over around five, Merlin called to say he'll be back by then. We have an hour. Do you think we could find something to keep us occupied till then?" Rhea was fairly certain they could, and wasted no time telling him so.

A few minutes before five they made a dash for the lodge, sharing the shelter of Alec's coat. Mrs Long ushered them into the parlour at the back of the house where a large coal fire was burning in an antiquated grate of polished black iron. Rhea had never seen a Yorkist Range in use before and would have thought they must all be in museums these days. The good dame snorted.

"The menfolk don't use this room over much, but I like to keep the range black-leaded. There's nowt like a good bread oven."

"Do you still use the range for that?" asked Rhea in surprise. Mrs Long answered by opening the black door of the oven. On one shelf was a tray of scones, on the other were two cob loaves, nicely browned, which she picked up with a tea towel, rapping the bottom of each loaf smartly with her knuckles. On the floor of the oven was a flat round loaf which she treated in similar manner. "If it sounds hollow, it's done."

"Yes, I remember my grandmother teaching me that when I was a little girl, though she used an ordinary oven."

"Well," replied Mrs Long, wrapping the loaves in clean cloths and picking up the tray of scones, "you were born down south, Miss Rhea." Alec held the door for her to pass while Rhea held her lip firmly between her teeth, not daring to catch Alec's eye, until the housekeeper had departed.

"That told me, didn't it?" she chuckled. Alec grinned in sympathy.

"You can't help being a 'foreigner', love." The playful condescension in his voice earned him a thump from his beloved. "Anyway, she must have decided to forgive you that piece of misfortune as she has dropped the 'Mrs Marchant' in favour of 'Miss Rhea'."

"Yes, I noticed! It made me feel about ten years old! It is a little incongruous given my age." Rhea smiled at the mental image she conjured. "Still, if Mrs Long is on my side, I think I can face anything. She is formidable enough to put the fear of God into a dragon!"

"Lord, that's one thing I hope we don't have to face!" The two were sobered by the thought which only a few days ago would have been no more than an idle comment.

A commotion in the hall announced the return of their friends. The couple in the parlour had only a few moments to wait before Jamie bounced in, grinning like the Cheshire cat.

"Hello, you two. Had a good day?"

"Yes thanks, Jamie." Alec replied for both of them. "What have you been up to this afternoon? You seem rather pleased with yourself." Jamie simply winked and tapped the side of his nose with his forefinger.

"Perhaps if we showed you what we found in Leeds you will understand." Merlin walked into the room. He was not alone but Rhea's cry was all the explanation Alec needed.

"Anna! What are you doing here?" Answers could wait, as mother and daughter flew at each other and embraced.

"It's a long story, darling," Anna's eyes, large and vividly blue, were sparkling with amusement. "But neither as long nor as interesting as the one Jamie has been telling me on the way from the airport. You have been busy while I've had my back turned, haven't you?" Something in her tone made Rhea glance sharply at Jamie, who was studiously examining the ceiling. Just what had the young man been saying?

Anna turned to Alec and held out her hand, her mother's smile lighting up her face and a decidedly mischievous glint in her eyes. Alec took the outstretched hand and found the grip to be surprisingly firm. The candid sapphire eyes regarded him steadily and he wondered whether she would disapprove of his love for Rhea, or resent him for intruding on her father's place.

"You must be Alec and I'm very glad to meet you. I've heard a lot about you in the past few days." Given the short time the group had been together and the even shorter time since Anna's arrival, this remark struck Rhea as rather odd.

"Past few days? How come?" she asked her daughter, then catching sight of Merlin's face she guessed the answer to the riddle. "Do you happen to know someone by the name of Heilyn?"

"Oh yes," Anna chuckled, "we've met. Rachel was offered a job singing solo in Vichy; Louisa has got engaged to Jean-Michel and gone to meet his parents in Villefranche and I was at a loose end. Heilyn turned up in the park one day and started talking. You seemed to be having more fun here than I was in France at that point, so I thought I'd skip back across the Channel and join in. If you'll have me, of course?" She spoke lightly, but the tone was earnest. "Jamie and Merlin have filled in the latest details since they picked me up. I rang to speak to you, but Merlin wanted you to rest today and volunteered to pick me up himself. I think I have understood the urgency and danger involved." Anna reached out and captured her mother's hand in hers. "Merlin won't allow me to get involved without your permission, and I would like your blessing too."

Rhea remembered the terror of the Barguest and the violence of the trolls. This was her daughter, her child, the precious life given into her care.

Anna was no longer a baby, but a woman grown, with fire in her eyes and who had already proved her courage and resilience over the last three years. There was something else here too, Rhea felt, conscious that four pairs of eyes were watching for her reaction and her answer. Firmly dismissing her fears, Rhea lifted her free hand and let her daughter's long, red-gold hair fall through her fingers,

"You have carried fire all your life, my dearest, Now, I think, you have a task as Bearer of Flame. For what it's worth, you have always had my blessing in whatever you have done and have made me always proud." Anna said nothing, simply hugged her mother. Jamie and Alec shared a glance which spoke volumes about their pride in the mother, while Merlin sniffed hastily and made much of blowing his nose.

Chapter Twelve

ANNA

Mrs Long stood at the door of the parlour. She rapidly assessed the situation and, depositing the tray on the sideboard, marched off to bring an extra set of crockery for the unexpected guest, muttering under her breath. She returned a few minutes later and Jamie offered to help her with the rest of the tea things, hoping to smooth any ruffled feathers with an explanation of the young lady's identity.

"Miss Marchant 'phoned this morning, Sissie, after you had gone out. She's going to stay with us for a while."

"That's Miss Rhea's lass?" Like Alec, Jamie recognised Rhea's promotion and was glad. "Well I never! She must have gotten that hair from her Dad. Here, you take the scones, lad, but mind you keep your fingers to yourself. Where is she staying? There isn't enough room at the cottage." The housekeeper pursed her lips, and Jamie wondered whether Mrs Long was aware that Rhea already had a part-time guest. Knowing the sergeant-major, he thought it likely that she was; little escaped her watchful eye. "I'll make her a room up, here at the Lodge, while you have tea."

The decisive comment made it quite clear that she would brook no argument, and Jamie, not averse to being in close proximity with a beauty like Anna, offered none.

Tea was served in the parlour and Rhea introduced her daughter to the housekeeper, who informed Merlin of her plans for putting Anna in the one of the guest rooms.

"Excellent, Mrs Long. Anna has been travelling for the last twenty-four hours so I'm sure she'll be glad of a hot bath and an early night." This snippet of information galvanised the housekeeper into action. Anna was pushed, almost bodily, into a chair and a small table placed at her side, laden with food and tea.

"You eat, Miss. There'll be a bath drawn in twenty minutes, and the sheets aired. Your Mam will show you the way. I'm sure."

"Thank you Mrs Long." Rhea bestowed a grateful smile on the good lady, who merely sniffed in her typical fashion before leaving the company to their tea.

"Now, Anna," said Merlin, "I think Alec and Rhea would both like to hear your side of the story." Anna settled herself with a sandwich and a cup of tea before beginning her tale.

"Everything has been arranging itself quite neatly for the past week or so, really," she began pensively. "Having met Heilyn, I suppose that should no longer surprise me. Rachel has a wonderful singing voice, as you know, Mum, and it's largely thanks to her that we have made our living so well while we've been travelling. Anyway, a couple of weeks ago, we arrived in Vichy. Louisa had met Jean-Michel a month before in Cannes, and they fell head over heels for each other. No-one, not even the two of them, I think, expected it to get so serious, but it did.

"They kept in contact by phone, all the time, and arranged to meet up in Vichy. Jean-Michel had a six week contract there and thought we could make a decent living all summer with the tourists. It was great! We explored or lazed on the banks of the Allier all day and sang in all the restaurants in the evenings. Louisa spent as much time as she could with Jean-Michel and a few days ago they announced that they were getting married. We all went out for a celebration dinner to a little place we hadn't known about before. They had a pianist, Rachel sang some Piaf and the owner offered her a job on the spot. Apparently, the regular singer had broken a leg and wouldn't be back for at least three months.

"Rachel, bless her, didn't want to take it and leave us in the lurch, but as Jean-Michel wanted to have Lou meet his family and was trying to persuade her to marry him quickly, we pushed her into accepting. Next day, Lou left for Villefranche and I started looking for a job, waitressing or something. The season having already started, I wasn't having much luck. I went and sat in the park; the squirrels are really tame and will come right up to you to be fed.

"One afternoon, a young boy came over and started talking to me in English. He said his name was Heilyn. I assumed he was with one of the families enjoying the park and listened to the fairytale he told me much as you would expect. It was only when the heroine of the story started to sound uncommonly like you, Mum, that I really started to take notice!

"Heilyn thought winding me up like that was hilarious, of course. Eventually, I got the truth out of him, after chasing him round the park. He changed into a squirrel just to prove a point; something about a sheep? He wouldn't go into details and told me I should ask Alec when I met him. Anyway, I thought it would be a good idea if I came home for a while to see for myself what was going on."

Alec had been looking fairly grim since the mention of sheep. Several pieces of the jigsaw suddenly fell into place for him and Merlin was worried as to how Alec would take having been so manipulated by the merry immortal. Jamie was valiantly trying to hold back his mirth until Rhea caught his eye. Rhea, too, had understood the oblique message and began to chuckle. Jamie lost his precious self-control and joined her, the pair of them shaking with laughter. Alec turned to Merlin rather ruefully.

"I think your brother is as good a shepherd as a sheep. He certainly had me penned up neatly." Merlin breathed a sigh of relief. It would have made a difficult task even harder if Alec had taken offence. His lips twitched and he smiled. Anna was a little perplexed by all this merriment and demanded that someone explain. Rhea was the first to regain some control and she took her daughter's hand, drawing her to the door.

"I think I will do the explaining, but not in front of this lot! Come on, your bath will be ready." Mother and daughter disappeared down the corridor towards the guest room. Quite how much Rhea told her daughter, the others never knew, but it was noticeable that Anna gave Alec some very searching looks when they met at dinner, later that evening.

Anna listened to her mother's story in silence as she lay in the steaming foam. Rhea perched on the linen chest, confiding in her daughter as a friend. Anna had just one question.

"Does he feel the same about you, darling?"

"Yes, I believe he does. Do you mind, dearest?" A very wet sponge was thrown with precision across the bathroom.

"Mind? I think it's wonderful!"

"Even if it turns out to be permanent? You won't mind him being in my life instead of your father?"

"Alec could never take Daddy's place, but I don't think he would want to. I've done a bit of growing up the last couple of years, Mum," said Anna, suddenly serious. "I know you loved Dad, but were you ever more than friends, really?"

"Yes, once upon a time we were, I think," Rhea answered with honesty, surprised at her daughter's perception.

"You and Alec share something different though, don't you? Even I could feel it. There is a fire there. He won't take Dad's place with you. He has his own place and it isn't the same. He won't take his place with me either, because he isn't Dad and I'm not a child anymore. I don't need a substitute and neither do you. Maybe it is a shame that you two didn't meet before I was born, but then, perhaps you and Alec needed time to grow up first. Go for it, Mum, with my blessing."

Rhea was astonished by Anna's logic and understanding. Her little girl had truly grown up and Rhea cherished the feeling of friendship that she found with her.

"Where did you acquire all this wisdom?" she asked, half in jest.

"They say wisdom comes with age, so all I had to do was study my dear old mother." Anna ducked to avoid the soggy return of the sponge. "Pass the towel, darling."

Back in Anna's room Rhea helped with the unpacking as Anna dressed in skin tight jeans and a long, chenille sweater the same blue as her eyes. She chatted all the while, filling in the details of Lou's romance and Rachel's singing. She also told tales of the fun the three friends had shared in Paris, Barcelona and Geneva. Rhea realised that if she had listened a week ago to stories of walking barefoot down the Champs Elysées at three in the morning, or impromptu jam sessions round a Swiss fountain, she would have envied her daughter. She would have regretted the youth and opportunity she herself had missed, envied the adventure of being alive and carefree.

Now all her thwarted daydreams had been made possible. She was fighting fairytale creatures in a quest where most of her allies were immortal. This was Romance on a legendary scale and she had also found love. Rhea felt truly alive, more clearly aware of the life of the world around her, which was part of her and of which she, herself, was a small but vital component.

For her part, Anna could not believe the change which had come over her mother. Her vitality glowed like a beacon and she had an air of self-confidence that had always been lacking before. In an unknowing echo of her mother's thoughts, she understood that Rhea had come back to life.

Since her father's death, Anna had come to see that her parents' marriage had been more of a habit than a true mating. When the comfortable routine had been cut from beneath her, Rhea had seemed rudderless and lost. Anna had been continually frustrated in her attempts to make her start building a new life.

It was with mixed feelings that she had left home to go to college, but it had proved a blessing in the end, as Rhea had felt so lonely in the big, detached house, that she had finally sold it and moved into a smaller flat. She had started painting, with Anna's encouragement, and gradually begun to find her feet in a world where all the rules seemed to have changed since she had last looked.

Now, finally, Anna thought she could begin to see what kind of a woman her mother really was, and she railed against the quiet conventions of suburbia which had kept Rhea cooped in a cage of mediocrity for twenty years.

If Alec Graham could create such a change, then Anna was very much in favour.

Rummaging through the papers at the bottom of the suitcase, Rhea came across a small packet which she held out to Anna.

"Oh yes, that's for you. I found it in a little antique shop in Paris and thought you'd like it. I was going to send it as a birthday present, but you can have it now instead."

Rhea opened the package and inside the crumpled tissue she found a small gold pendant. It was a single ribbon of rosy gold, twined around a central clouded moonstone shot with rainbows. Rhea was struck by the similarity in design to the ring which Merlin had given her.

"When did you buy this?"

"About six weeks ago, I suppose. Why?"

"Then I think we have been following a path laid out for us rather longer than we have realised." She held out her hand and allowed Anna to compare the two pieces of jewellery, the style so similar that both could have been wrought by the same hand. Anna cocked an eyebrow in query. "This ring is over fifteen hundred years old." Rhea told her daughter briefly of its origins, as it was not her tale to tell. "If you are ready, we should go and show this to Merlin. I think he will be interested."

Merlin was intrigued by the design of the cross which Anna had given her mother and examined it closely, even going so far as to look for a maker's mark with a magnifying glass.

"Well, well. Take a look at this, you two," he said, passing the golden pendant to the men. "It's a swastika. No, no," he smiled at Anna reassuringly, "it is not a Nazi symbol, but far older than even the historians can tell. It is curious that you should find this so far away and bring it back here, for up on the moor stands the Swastika Stone, one of only a handful in the world today.

"Think of an equal armed cross and spin it on a central point like a Catherine wheel. Imagine that the ends of the arms leave a trail, like a comet in flight as they move. Rotate the cross sunwise and the arms leave a trail following their movement. This is the swastika of the Old Ones, symbol of Light and Fire. The swastika Hitler adopted faces the opposite way, as if it spun counter-clockwise. He took the symbol of Light and perverted it, making it the darkest sigil of the age. It is not surprising that you did not realise what it was. The Nazi symbol was angular, while this flows in fluid curves.

"You, child, I believe, are to be the Bearer of Flame and holder of the Sword of Fire. I think it more than coincidence that this should be brought here. The pendant has no mark and could be any age. It is likely a copy of an older piece, though certainly similar in style to the ring you wear, Rhea. I believe we shall have to walk to the Swastika Stone on the moor in the very near future."

"Do we know what the next step should be yet?" Alec asked as he fastened the fine gold chain around his Rhea's neck.

"Unless the pendant is the only message, then no," Merlin replied, "but I shall make no decision on that tonight. There is one thing that should be done, though. Anna, you have now heard our story and much else besides from Heilyn. If you are still willing to join our company then there is the matter of your formal acceptance into the group. I shall not press you for a decision tonight, but I must say that all the signs point in your favour.

"Do not underestimate the dangers, they are as real as you have heard and I cannot say whether we will succeed or fail. The choice must be yours alone, child."

"I do not need any more time to decide, Merlin. My mind is made up and the more I hear, the more convinced I am of the rightness of what you are trying to do. I want to be a part of it and help in whatever small way I can."

Anna's eyes were clear and steady and there was neither doubt nor excitement on her face, simply a calm determination. Alec was struck by the resemblance between mother and daughter, not so much in feature as in courage. Merlin smiled and nodded, holding out his hand to the young woman before him.

"Then, child, as you are resolved on this, there is an introduction to be made." Anna looked round as if expecting to see another person in the room, but Merlin merely smiled and held her hand. "Rhea, would you bring the sword, my dear? Gentlemen…"

The mage gestured for the others to gather round him. He placed Rhea, bearing the sword, on his right hand and Anna on his left. Following his quiet voice into the void, they built the protective cone of white light, all except Anna finding the visualisation easier this time. Merlin instructed Rhea to hold the sword before her, the hilt forming a cross. This time, they recognised the shift in consciousness as they passed the portals to the Realm of Light.

Anna felt that she should fall to her knees before the Great One who received them, but she stood her ground as Merlin again spoke for the company.

"Here is the Flame-Bearer, last of the Champions. She gives herself unreservedly into the service of the Light. Wilt Thou give her Thy blessing?"

Merlin drew Anna forward and she was engulfed in the radiance of the Presence. She felt a sensation as if a giant Hand rested lightly upon the crown of her head. Suffused with joy and humility she came closer to the angels of her childhood dreams than she had believed possible this side of death. When Merlin spoke again, even his melodious voice sounded harsh amid the harmonies that seemed to hang in the very air around them.

"The Heart of Earth now holds the first of the Swords to be recovered. Rhea, hold out the blade." Rhea complied, raising the weapon before her. Light incandescent streamed from the Presence and hit the tip of the blade with a shock like lightning and she staggered under the weight of power. But she braced her feet firmly and stood, feeling the Light flow along the blade and through every fibre of her being, curling around her in blazing tendrils.

She felt the sword come alive in her hands, with life borrowed from her own, yet taking nothing from her, leaving her enriched and more vital than ever. She and the blade resonated with the same song of the soul. Gently the power eased, its final withdrawal as keen as loss. Rhea lowered the blade and sank to her knees, hugging the sword to her breast, exultant and exhausted.

Merlin allowed Rhea a moment to recover before beginning to reverse the ritual. However, they did not go immediately back to the cosy room they had left, but found themselves hovering over a desolate landscape, seeing with the eyes of flight.

Jamie felt sick as vertigo clutched at him; Anna and Rhea were still too overcome with awe to take in their surroundings, but Alec was suddenly alert. He felt that he should recognise the scene, but it began to fade almost immediately. He fixed as much of the topography in his mind as he could.

There was a mountain at the centre of the scene, cloud-wreathed and hostile, with the valley below a patchwork of dry stone walls and velvet green. He had a feeling that he should know this place well, but had no time to identify it before they were back in the warm normality of the Lodge.

Merlin wound down the dome of light and gave each of them his own blessing, finally laying his hands on Rhea's head where she still knelt cradling the sword. She seemed to have a long way to come back and her eyes held a faraway look, taking several long seconds to focus. Alec was concerned that she should have gone so far from them and looked to Merlin for reassurance.

"It is a baptism of sorts," the mage murmured, "a unique experience. You will understand when your own time comes." His voice brought them home. "Now, as Mrs Long has left for the night, who is going to volunteer to make us all a cup of tea?"

It was Anna, accompanied by Jamie, who went to raid the housekeeper's domain in search of tea and biscuits, while Alec gently disengaged Rhea's hands from the sword and laid it aside.

"Alec, did you recognise that last scene?"

"Sort of, Merlin. I have the feeling I know it well, but the perspective was rather novel, you must admit!" Alec replied, his arm lightly round his lady's waist. "Any ideas?"

"We'll ask Jamie when he comes back. How are you feeling, my dear?"

"A little dazed," replied Rhea. "It was very different this time. Still awesome, but the sword was vibrating, as if it had gone home somehow." Her voice held a question and Merlin did his best to give her a reply.

"Although the swords are real in a material sense, you could say that they do not exist in this world until they are called. Given where you found it, you'll have gathered that the Sword of Earth has not been hanging in mid-air for millennia, halfway down a Yorkshire pot-hole." He chuckled at the mental picture he had conjured. "The swords exist everywhere and nowhere until need calls them into becoming, then they appear as necessity and circumstance dictates."

Alec considered the old man's words.

"Does that mean that they can simply appear anywhere?"

"In a sense, yes. But they will only appear in the right 'anywhere' for the given age of the world. We could not, for instance, look for the swords in any other place but this as the need is here and not elsewhere. We have to determine the whereabouts of each sword but we will only find them in the right place. By the same token, the swords cannot be in the right place until we have found them. A paradox, if you like.

"Without the swords, we are just a group of ordinary people, only with the blades do we become the Champions of Light. Yet, until we are the Champions, the essence that is the swords cannot manifest in this time and place." Merlin smiled and shrugged his shoulders. "I hope you can make some sense of that." Rhea smiled back serenely, intuitively understanding the paradox, but Alec's more logical mind wrestled still with the enigma. Finally, he too shrugged, imitating Merlin's gesture. What he could not grasp, he would take on trust and hope that experience would bring enlightenment.

The rattle of crockery and muted laughter heralded the return of the younger members of the company. Jamie backed in, bearing a laden tray and holding the door for Anna who followed him with a large brown teapot. The tray was stacked in a business-like manner with big earthenware mugs, plates and one of Mrs Long's fruit loaves. Jamie, at least, was ready for supper.

Mugs of tea were distributed and slabs of the rich cake passed around, Anna complaining loudly about the unfair advantage Jamie appeared to possess, being able to consume such large quantities of food and still remain slim. The banter between the youngsters did much to lighten the atmosphere and Merlin watched in approval, a smile hovering round the corners of his mouth. His chosen Champions had seemed to melt effortlessly into a coherent and harmonious group which boded well for their work together.

Alec asked Jamie if he had recognised that last scene. The young man finished the mouthful of cake before replying.

"Sorry, Alec, the flying took me by surprise. I wasn't concentrating. Why don't you sketch what you saw?"

"Good Lord, I'm no artist!"

"Good idea, though," said Merlin. "Perhaps if we can get the bare bones on paper, Rhea can flesh them out for us." The two went to the desk and began scribbling down their impressions. The sketch was produced some minutes later and given to Rhea.

"See what you can come up with tomorrow," Merlin asked. "I don't think we have much time to waste and we really need to know where the next sword is to be looked for." Rhea studied the rough drawing, something tugging at the corners of her mind. She was very tired and was finding it hard to focus.

"Okay, I'll do my best."

"Now, children," said the mage," I think we should all retire. Anna has had a long journey today and a stranger one this evening." He smiled at Anna as he spoke. "It is nearly midnight and we would all benefit from a decent night's sleep. Alec, will you walk Rhea back to the cottage? I shall escort Anna to her room, or these two will be talking all night." Anna and her mother exchanged a rueful glance, Merlin's supposition being essentially correct.

"I'll see to the tea things before I go," Rhea offered.

"Actually, you won't." Rhea found herself relieved of the tray by a resolute Jamie. "Take her to bed, Alec, she looks all in." A gurgle of irreverent laughter greeted this remark and Jamie grinned, realising he could have chosen his words a little better. Alec, however, smiled and took Rhea by the elbow, marching her towards the door.

"That is probably the most sensible suggestion you have made all day, my friend." He smiled, his eyes dancing at Jamie's gaffe. "Say goodnight, Rhea." She met her daughter's eyes and found herself outnumbered.

"Goodnight." Alec carried her off and really, she admitted to herself, she was too tired to object.

The rain had stopped and the night was chill and clear, all the stars of heaven casting their silver light on the moors as the couple walked back to the cottage together. Alec had his arm around her waist and Rhea felt completely at peace.

"It's a beautiful night. It almost seems a shame to go in." Alec agreed with her, but he had seen the exhaustion on her face and was concerned. She had been through a great deal over the past few days and by all accounts, their task had barely begun.

"When we have more time I will take you up on the moor one night to watch the stars. It's too late tonight."

"Will you come in for a while?" They had reached the door and Rhea turned to him, the pale light illuminating her upturned face and her hands sliding into his.

"If I did, I wouldn't go home again."

"And?" The invitation in her voice was as unmistakable as it was irresistible and they crossed the threshold together.

Their loving that night was tender and gentle. Time no longer mattered. They were so new to each other and to love that every touch, light as the caress of a butterfly's wing, brought them to breathless wonder, spiralling ever upward together toward the Light that had given them the gift of belonging. Rhea felt the same sensation of being inundated with luminous life that she had felt in the presence of the angelic being and realised that somehow these things were linked and part of a greater whole.

Much later they lay in each other's arms, bodies touching and legs entwined. With one hand Rhea traced the contours of his chest and the silken skin of his stomach. Alec lifted a hand to touch her cheek and encountered the warm dampness of tears.

"What's wrong, love?" A tiny shake of the head was his only answer and concern made his voice hoarse.

"Oh Alec, you feel so nice to touch and this is so beautiful .and it all feels so right." The woman laid her hand on his heart. "Thank you."
"It is I who should thank you. You have brought me peace. It may sound an odd thing to say, but something in me has come home." Alec searched for the right words, but Rhea, it seemed, understood.

"I think we have both come home, love."

Chapter Thirteen

TAKING FLIGHT

Morning brought clear skies and sunlight dancing on the dew drenched moor. Alec was first to rouse and he took time to savour the sensation of waking beside the sleeping woman. Love for her flowed through him and he thanked all the gods that they had found each other. Rhea was smiling in her sleep and looked so relaxed and peaceful that Alec had no desire to disturb her. Carefully he slid out of bed and headed naked for the bathroom, pausing to fill the kettle on his way. Very quietly he showered and, clad in the pink towelling robe he had found, proceeded to make toast and coffee, laying a pretty tray for his lady.

Alec found he derived great pleasure from the homely task. He was a competent cook and could look after himself adequately, but preparing the simple meal for Rhea felt utterly different and far more satisfying than his culinary efforts usually did.

He paused by the sitting room table to select a flower from the vase to brighten the tray and noticed the painting Rhea had been working on the previous day. With amazement he scrutinised the scene. Here, unmistakeably, was the landscape he had glimpsed on the return from the Inner Realms last night. The sphinx-like mountain, seen in profile this time, was immediately identifiable and he wondered that he had not recognised it before.

Once again it was Rhea who had given them the clue they needed and Alec was left to wonder that none of them had realised the significance of her art before.

A soft murmur from the bedroom drew his attention and, picking up the tray he went through.

"Good morning, love." He placed the tray on the chest of drawers and bent to kiss Rhea. "I've made coffee. Would you like to sit up while I pour?"

"Alec, you're an angel! I haven't had breakfast in bed since Anna was about ten." Rhea ran her fingers through her tousled curls and sat up, pulling the sheets up over her breasts, the thin cotton doing little to disguise their soft curves and much to disturb Alec. Her body was no longer that of a young girl, but was beautiful in its maturity, though he thought that she was a little too thin and wondered just how well she had bothered to eat while she had been alone.

His jaw tightened at the idea of his woman alone and uncared for. A few weeks of good Yorkshire food… and Alec knew Mrs Long well enough to have no qualms on that score… would soon fill out the hollows and soften the angles of the slight frame.

He poured coffee and found Rhea grinning impishly.

"The colour suits you," she said, running a critical eye over his attire, "though perhaps a few sizes too small." Alec raised his eyes to heaven in mock exasperation delighting in the banter. Any rejoinder he would have made, however was forestalled as she added, "Perhaps you should bring a few things round later that would fit you better."

"You wouldn't mind?"

"No, love, it would be nice to have something of you here when you are not."

"I think something of me will be with you wherever we are. I love you very much, you know." His voice was rather husky as Rhea rescued the coffee cup and placed it on the bedside table.

"Are you certain of that, Alec? It is not something that has been imposed on you by the extraordinary circumstances in which we have met?"

The question in her eyes showed her fear that this would be a transient thing. Alec looked into the clear eyes and tried to pour his soul into his reply that she might see how necessary she had become to his life.

"I don't know why, or how, but if we have been pushed together then I thank God for it. I love you with all that I am and with you, for the first time in my life, I feel whole. I cannot imagine a future without you and if you'll have me, I don't intend to try."

She caught his hand and carried it to her cheek. On the third finger of her left hand the narrow gold band was a poignant symbol of loss and reason enough for her fears.

"Rhea," suddenly diffident, "When this is over, when you are sure of me, will you be my wife? You don't have to answer right now, just think about it." Rhea's eyes widened in surprise. She had not envisaged this possibility and it was a few moments before she could answer, moments which felt like ages to Alec.

"Yes, love." She smiled, radiantly confident at last. "Oh yes, love, please. If you want me."

And breakfast was forgotten as Alec showed her just how much he wanted her.

Jamie and Anna, meanwhile, were getting along famously, ribbing each other with the ease usually born of long friendship and delighting Merlin with their banter. Jamie had taken Anna up onto the moor after breakfast, returning in time for lunch. Both were dressed in jeans and T-shirt but there the resemblance ended. Jamie wore his clothes in the most casual manner and was rarely seen smartly dressed. His fair hair seemed to find its own style after having careless fingers dragged hurriedly through it and the boyish face shone as if freshly scrubbed.

Anna, however, gave an impression of casual elegance. The soft shirt and narrow jeans enhanced the slender curves and the rose-gold hair, parted in the middle, fell in a burnished stream around her face.

To Merlin's eye there was something about the pair that was clean and wholesome. Opposite in so many ways, they yet shared an indefinable quality which, the old man knew, came of their commitment to the Light. He saw the same signs written indelibly on the faces of Rhea and Alec when they entered as lunch was drawing to an end.

"Afternoon, Merlin. Any coffee left?"

"Only if this greedy boy has overlooked it," quipped Anna. "He's finished everything else!" She passed over two steaming cups as she spoke.

"Rhea has brought a painting for you to see, Merlin." He nodded to Rhea to show the misty water colour to the mage. "We ought to have brought it over earlier, but we got side-tracked." Rhea flushed a rosy pink.

"It's a very strong image, Rhea. Well executed and faithful to the landscape."

"What landscape? Alec wouldn't say a great deal till I'd shown it to you. I just made it up yesterday. At least, I thought I did."

Merlin passed the picture to Jamie and awaited his response.

"It's Pen-y-Ghent, isn't it?" the young man said. "One of the Three Peaks."

"Yes, along with Ingleborough and Whernside. This is the place we saw from above last night." Merlin looked at Alec for confirmation.

"Yes, I recognised it as soon as I saw the painting this morning," he replied. "I have climbed up there many times when I was younger. It is a beautiful walk on a fine day, but a damned dangerous one in bad weather. I think we need to go there."

"I'm inclined to agree." Merlin wiped the remains of lunch from his moustache with a napkin. "Do you know that Pen-y-Ghent is supposed to mean 'hill of the winds'? Very appropriate for the location of the Sword of Air." Jamie whistled softly at this revelation. "I think we will need to keep a close eye on Rhea's work. It seems her talents extend rather deeper than we have been giving her credit for. My apologies Rhea, I should have realised sooner."

Rhea waved away the apology while her daughter demanded an explanation.

"Rhea has managed to show us the way every time we've been stuck," proffered Jamie. He then launched into a description of the various events where Rhea's gifts had played a key role, ending with a dramatic account of their adventure at Trollers Gill.

While Anna listened, fascinated, to Jamie's graphic recital, Rhea took the opportunity to ask Merlin about the mountain.

"I should have liked to go today, if possible. It's a fair way though and a hard walk at the end of it. Let me think a while."

The old man withdrew into his own thoughts for several minutes before finally shaking his head with a sigh.

"Well, I have an idea, but I shall need some help and Jamie's not going to like it. He hates flying." Alec and Rhea exchanged puzzled glances.

"I don't think there's an airfield in the vicinity and you couldn't land a helicopter up on the summit, even if we could charter one at such short notice, " Alex observed. "Just what have you got in mind, old friend?"

"A slightly risky solution, but one which would save us a lot of time if we can pull it off." He rose and walked to the door. "Give me half an hour to see if I can work it out and then I'll explain." He left the room and went in search of advice.

The four who remained went out into the sunlight, trying to work out what Merlin was planning and not progressing past Jamie's flat refusal to consider a helicopter ride. His fear of flying had no rational basis, but it was very real and Anna spent a good deal of time trying to understand his problem and find a solution. Twenty minutes later, however, Merlin was able to reassure Jamie that no helicopters would be involved.

"I've asked for some help to gain us a little time. We have to be up on the moor shortly, so go and get some decent footwear and coats, we will be out late again, I expect. He held up his hand to forestall any questions, indicating Mrs Long who was clearing the dining room, windows wide open, just behind them. "Rhea, you must bring the sword. Come to the library when you are ready to collect it. It is time you began to get used to the feel of it anyway."

The party dispersed in the direction of their rooms, with Alec following Rhea back to the cottage.

Half an hour later Merlin led the party into a small hollow on the moor, hidden behind a great boulder left stranded an age ago by a glacier. The company were waiting for Merlin to explain when the air bent and shimmered in the way that all except Anna had now seen several times. The tall figure of the Horned One stood before them, majestic in his nakedness. All were moved to bow before the god who inclined the tines of his antlers in acknowledgement.

"Well met again, my son. I see you have found the Bearer of Flame. It is good that your company should be finally complete, and this one is very fair." Cernunnos ran appreciative eyes over the slim figure and rose-gold hair.

"She is my daughter, Forest Lord," said Rhea, stepping protectively in front of Anna, who was staring at the sun bronzed god in astonished awe. There was steel in Rhea's voice to match the blade in her hand and the god threw back his head and laughed aloud.

"Your pardon, my lady! I am a hunter, not a poacher, but her beauty is that of the rising sun on misty waters. I am not unmoved." That much was evident, but Rhea carefully averted her eyes and acknowledged his bow with a nod of her head, wary still. Her daughter's frank admiration of the virile figure before them did not help allay her fears at all and she was glad when Merlin turned the conversation to their more immediate problems.

"Heilyn will have told you what I have in mind I suppose? Will you help us?"

"Yes, I can get you there in time, but only as far as the Giant's Grave. After that you will be too close to your goal and I may not interfere. Will that be of use?"

"Father, that would be good. I have a feeling we need to be there today. Something is nagging at the edges of my mind and it is unsettling." Merlin cast an inquiring glance at his sire, who shook his head.

"My son, you must discover the nature of this for yourself. For you are under threat and must make haste to recover the swords.

"Now let us take thought. The Sword of Earth must be carried, so size and strength will be required. The sword is beyond me. Eagles, perhaps?"

"Yes, range and stamina and the talons for the blade. But five would be conspicuous these days."

"Yes, they have diminished, I know." There was infinite sadness in his voice. "What would you suggest?"

"I shall go in my usual guise, Rhea must carry the sword. Something smaller, perhaps, for the others?" Merlin suggested. Jamie had been following this cryptic conversation with growing suspicion. And he didn't like it one bit.

"Oh no, I'm not flying anywhere!" The young man looked rather green and Rhea wondered whether it was the thought of the flight or the manner of it that worried him the most.

"Don't worry, Jamie, I will not ask you to fly." Alec, watching the old man closely, detected a distinct twinkle in his eye. "Now, I have asked my sire's help in transforming most of you into birds. We will get to the mountain far quicker and it's the only way we'll get there today with the sword and still be at the summit before nightfall. I can hold my own shape with ease, but the presence of the sword complicates the magic. You can have complete faith in my father's powers; they are infinitely greater than mine.

"Rhea must carry the sword. Take a firm grip and don't let go. This will not hurt and you will soon get the hang of it. Alec, stay close to her. Anna, can you take hold of Jamie? Yes, that's right. Don't worry lad, I won't give you wings." There was panic in Jamie's eyes, and laughter in the peat brown eyes of the mage betrayed the fact that he was plotting something.

"Father?"

"May the wind carry you lightly!"

The air around Rhea took on an opalescent sheen and she felt herself melt into the light. When the shifting rainbows cleared the watchers saw a golden eagle, proud and majestic, looking back at them with Rhea's eyes. The eagle grasped the heavy sword firmly in the wicked talons and sprang aloft, its flight laboured and erratic until Rhea realised that the form had its own understanding of the laws of flight and she gave herself up to the pleasure of the experience.

Moments later she was joined by another eagle which she somehow recognised as Alec. The two soared gracefully above the hollow, watching the group on the ground. Rhea saw Cernunnos whisper something to Anna who started, before nodding her assent and melting into the form of a peregrine falcon. Jamie, visibly panicked, now shrank down to the form of a field mouse.

Merlin and his father both laughed, though not unkindly, as the falcon held the mouse firmly in her talons. There was a squeak and the mouse went limp. Anna flew up to circle with the others. Merlin too had taken the falcon shape and, after flying once around his father's head in thanks, soared up to join his companions.

Rhea never forgot the wonder of that flight. The breeze in her feathers, the power in her wings and the soaring ease with which she rode the wind. The eagle's eyes showed her colours that she had never seen as the earth curved away beneath her and always afterwards, her paintings held a luminous and unearthly quality as she strove to depict what she had seen.

The flight was not a long one, a mere thirty miles as the eagle flew, to the north-west, out over the lonely moorland towards the Three Peaks. Flying high enough to avoid curious eyes, they passed through cloud and turbulent air and Rhea wondered how Jamie was faring. It was almost wicked of Merlin to have tricked the boy like that, but Rhea knew that Jamie had to be brought along somehow. He was a necessary member of the party.

They were flying lower now, over the massive limestone cliffs of Malham Cove, which Rhea recognised, the Peaks already visible from their unique vantage point. Merlin began to wheel downward in a fabulous display of aerial wizardry. He landed and the shimmering air settled to reveal the mage, once more in human form. Rhea wondered what exactly the mage's true form really was.

Anna and the two eagles followed more sedately, alighting on the ground at Merlin's feet. First Rhea, then Alec was restored and they watched as Anna and the mouse shimmered back to their accustomed shapes. Whether through an oversight, or Merlin's sense of the ridiculous, Anna still had a firm grip on Jamie who sprawled in an ungainly heap at her feet. Anna bent over the quivering man.

"You okay, Jamie?" she asked, full of concern for her erstwhile passenger. She was answered by a shuddering groan. He turned towards her, an unhealthy green tinge to his skin and let his head drop onto her shoulder, his face buried in the rose-gold cascade.

Anna looked helplessly at Merlin who smiled encouragingly and turned away, studying the remains of the long barrow that was called the Giant's Grave. There seemed little help forthcoming from her mother and

Alec, who were hugging each other exultantly, so she bent her head to Jamie and held him close while the shuddering subsided.

"Any better?" she asked .

"I thought you were going to drop me," came the muffled answer. Anna gave a gurgle of laughter.

"I wouldn't have done that, though I did nearly eat you."

"What?" The casual remark jerked the young man upright.

"Well, I suppose it was the avian instinct," she apologised. "If the instinct to fly goes with the form, then I imagine others must too. Falcons do eat rodents, you know. I was enjoying the flight and began feeling peckish. I'm sorry."

Jamie got to his feet, the green effectively banished.

"Merlin!" The cry would have carried for miles and the venerable mage turned to face him, an expression of supreme innocence on the ancient face.

"Hmm?"

"She wanted to eat me!"

"Ah, I should have thought of that. Never mind."

"Never mind? Never mind!" Jamie spluttered, at a loss for words.

"I'll bear it in mind next time."

"There will be no next time, Merlin, not ever."

"No? Oh well, it will have to be something inedible then, not a rodent." Jamie had the distinct impression that the old man was teasing him, but the shocking ride had robbed him of his normal resources, so he settled for a noncommittal grunt and stomped away. Anna, at least, was sympathetic and he became her escort.

The party was standing amid the ruins of an Iron Age long barrow; a mound built over a passage grave. The stone had long since been carted away to provide building materials for the local populace. Before them stretched the long climb to the summit of Pen-y-Ghent, the Hill of Winds.

"Shall we get on?" asked Alec. "The weather looks pretty unstable and we should try and get up there before it breaks." Merlin nodded his assent and the party set off at a brisk pace towards the mountain.

The climb was no worse than a strenuous walk, but the eroded paths and scattered limestone made the going difficult. The country around them, however, was magnificent and Rhea drank in the beauty. The grass was the colour of emeralds, growing lush between the limestone boulders and bounded by the ageless dry stone walls whose foundations had been laid by the earliest settlers in this wild region. Eventually the green gave way to all the muted tones of grey as they climbed the steep path, passing streams and noisy little waterfalls. At one point they passed a small waterfalls falling deep into a crevasse, which, Alec told them, was called Hunt Pot, a sheer drop of nearly three hundred feet straight into the bowels of the hill.

By the time the party had reached the summit, the sky was overcast. Great dark clouds roiled above and around them, evidence of the dramatic changes the local weather was apt to inflict on walkers. It was as dark as night and Rhea, stumbling under the weight of the sword she carried, could only be glad that they found no more treacherous holes like Hunt Pot to swallow them.

They stopped to catch their breath after the arduous climb, sitting on the rocks of the summit with the cloud swirling around them, creating an island upon which they felt isolated from the ordinary life in the valley below.

"Do you know where we should start looking?" Alec asked Merlin.

"No, I think we should follow your instincts on this, Alec. Close your eyes and try to feel the sword with your mind." Alec obeyed, but after several minutes of strained silence he shook his head and opened his eyes. His logical mind failed to feel the pull of the blade.

"It's no use, I'm afraid. I really don't know what the sword is supposed to feel like." Merlin beckoned to Rhea and asked her to use the Sword of Earth to guide Alec. She stood before him, the blade in her hands. Alec put his arms around her and placed his hands over hers, so that both were grasping the hilt. They stood thus for a short while, then Alec came alert. There was a distinct pull, like the attraction of a magnet. Rhea had stiffened in his arms and he knew that she, too, had felt it. Wordlessly, the two followed the pull of the swords, waking blindly in the direction of the sheer cliff. Merlin gestured for Anna and Jamie to follow them, holding a finger to his lips for silence.

The strange cortege moved inexorably closer to the cliff edge. Jamie was becoming seriously worried that in the poor visibility they would go too far. At last they stopped. Alec opened his eyes and looked ahead of into the gloom.

"It is out there somewhere, I can feel it, but I can't see it. Jamie, hold my feet." Jamie complied as Alec threw himself flat on the stony ground and peered out over the cliff. "There is a pillar of rock detached from the cliff face. It must be the Sentinel. I have to get there somehow. It is almost impossible from up here, even with proper climbing gear, as the rock is friable. I have to try, though."

"Yes, I think you must, but with speed and great care. Look!" Merlin pointed to the billowing clouds and fear struck them like a knife in the darkness.

"There are faces in the clouds!" cried Anna. "Nightmare faces." They could all see them. Flying slugs with vampire teeth, great toad-like creatures with human heads and inhuman eyes, disembodied screams issuing from faceless lips. The wind was rising, sweeping across the hilltop like callous laughter, mocking and hideous. Anna huddled close to Jamie, who held her tight against him.

"Now, Alec, go now!" Merlin shouted above the noise. Alec made a lunge for the edge of the cliff, but a vast squid-like creature with a grinning skull thrust out a tentacle to snare him. Rhea darted forward without thought or hesitation, wielding the sparkling blade like a scythe, hacking at the tentacles. But this creature was born of storm clouds and evil, intent upon its prey. Every severed limb was replaced as soon as it fell. Rhea wept with fury and frustration as she battled the monster.

"Help me, Jamie, help me!" Jamie picked up a rock from the ground and hurled it with all his strength at the evil skull. He was running towards Rhea before it struck home. The creature reeled and Alec took advantage of the brief respite to leap recklessly out towards the Sentinel. Anna screamed and began hurling rocks, the only weapon to hand, as Merlin started to run towards the beleaguered group, power gathering around him like a cloak.

Jamie hurled another rock as Rhea slashed at the smoky tentacles. Her blow went wide and she slipped, the sword flailing in panic. Anna screamed again as Jamie made a dive for Rhea. His hand closed round the sword, the keen blade slicing into the flesh as Rhea disappeared over the edge of the cliff. Tears streaked the shocked young face as Jamie transferred the sword to his left hand and screamed at their attacker.

"Come on, you bastard! Come and get me." He braced himself for the onslaught and as the creature drew near he launched himself in a frenzy of grief, slashing and hacking, the great sword ablaze in his hand.

A streak of blue flame hit the writhing monstrosity and it squirmed and shrivelled like a sliced worm. Jamie glanced up and saw Alec atop the Sentinel with a Sword in his hands, limned in blue fire. A mighty warrior, it seemed, armed against evil. Again and again the bolts hit home until the creature howled and fled into the darkness that spawned it. The two men sank to their knees, exhausted by the fray and stunned by the nauseating evil the creature had exuded.

"Mother!" Anna's desperate cry broke the momentary silence and Jamie dragged himself to his feet, running to where Anna leaned precariously over the crumbling edge.

"Where is Merlin?"

Anna pointed over the cliff. "He went down there. I can't see anything."

"Merlin! Merlin!" Jamie yelled. The only answer was the screech of a falcon. Alec scrambled back from the Sentinel and threw himself down beside Jamie.

"What's wrong, where is Rhea?" Jamie shook his head and indicated the sheer drop from the cliff.

"Merlin went after her. We don't know what is happening." Alec was as white faced as the two youngsters, but while Jamie wept silently and Anna sobbed in fear, Alec felt only a cold scream building deep inside.

Seconds dragged by like hours and Alec had never felt so alone and helpless. If Rhea had fallen from the cliff then there was little chance that she could survive. The screaming fear that had been writhing in his guts exploded in a storm of blue fire. The air crackled with electricity and smelled of ozone. Jamie and Anna, terrified by this display of power, were thrown back from the edge. Rocks cracked and snapped, a hundred years of erosion in a heartbeat. The ground convulsed beneath their feet and Anna clutched at Jamie for support as a maelstrom built around them.

"Windlord, hold!" The booming voice reached Alec even through his impotent grief and the storm diminished. He spun towards the voice and found himself facing a man-like creature as tall as an oak tree. "Hold fast!" Alec banked his flames to a mere glimmer, yet he held himself tall and defiant before the giant.

"Who are you to question my action?" Jamie hardly recognised his friend in the stern figure.

"Little man, I am the guardian of this place and was called from my rest by the Keeper of Light."

"Merlin? What do you know of him? Where is he?" There was a sound like the rumble of distant thunder, but holding no threat and Jamie realised the giant was laughing.

"Patience, little man. I know much of the Keeper, more than you will ever learn in your short life. I knew him before the wolves left the mountain, when eagles wheeled and wild boar roamed."

"Do you know where he is now? He went over the edge to help a fallen comrade and we cannot find them. We would be grateful for your help." Alec, it seemed, had finally regained some control and a little common sense. If Merlin had vanished and yet called this creature, there had to be a reason for it and his heart leaped with hope. The ground beneath them vibrated to the sound of the giant's merriment.

"I swallowed your friends. It seemed better than to let two lives go to waste on these barren rocks." Jamie saw Alec stiffen again and take a firm grip on the sword, ready to attack even this towering being for his lady's sake. He reminded Jamie of the knights out of the old stories his grandmother used to tell him as a boy.

"Peace, manling, I have done them no harm. Even now your companions are very close."

Alec was confused, grief and fear had clouded his judgement but it was beginning to make a kind of sense to Jamie.

"Alec!" he shouted. "Put up your sword and listen." The grotesque face of the giant, which seemed to have been hewn from the weathered rock of the plateau, creased in a twisted grin. He raised his fist and brought it down with a single mighty blow, setting the earth rippling and creaking around them as if no longer solid. A jagged crack opened in the rock between Alec and the giant, and as the earthquake settled the begrimed head of Merlin emerged from the rift.

Chapter Fourteen

WINDLORD

As the cliff edge crumbled beneath her feet, Rhea made one last, desperate effort to thrust the sword into the ground. Someone caught the blade and called her name but the momentum of her fall was too great to be stopped by any human agency. In blind panic she tore at the cliff as she fell, dislodging a shower of stones and earth which stung her face. Each second seemed interminable and she wished it were over, the pain of losing Anna and Alec greater than anything her body had to bear. She had seen the face of this cliff all too clearly from the air and she knew there would be nothing to halt her fall. She would be falling for the rest of her life. Which would not be long.

It was the shriek of the falcon which made her open her eyes. Merlin's avian form was hovering before her face and she was no longer plummeting down the mountain. She was falling still, too fast for safety she realised, but maybe, just maybe, slow enough for hope. The falcon's imperious shriek carried a note of command. Suddenly her back struck something hard and she heard no more.

When Rhea opened her eyes it was to a silent, aching blackness. Her breath came in ragged gasps and she could see nothing. The pain was almost welcome. She did not think death would hurt this much. The lack of sight frightened her. She moved experimentally and groaned as a shaft of agony lanced her ankle.

"Ah, you are back, my dear. Wait a moment." Merlin's voice in the blackness was the most welcome sound she had ever heard. There was a soft whoosh and a pale golden light bloomed in the mage's hands, illuminating his face, the peat brown eyes full of concern. "My dear child, can you ever forgive me? You seem to be taking the worst of this fight once again." As he spoke, he set the dancing flame on the ground beside her and began to examine her injuries with infinite care.

"There is nothing to forgive, Merlin. I'm just glad you saved me." The old man's familiar chuckle did much to steady her.

"I didn't. You will have to save your thanks for a friend of mine. This mountain is the home of one of the Elder Race, Ogmios. He opened a door for us and let us in. Nothing moves on this mountain without his knowledge."

"He is allowed to intervene?"

"He is as old as the mountain itself. Indeed, you could say he is the mountain in a way. There are few left to command him. We are now in his domain and safe until you are able to move again." His probing hands found the damaged ankle and he worked his healing magic, coaxing the swelling to manageable proportions and soothing the worst of the bruising.

While he worked, Rhea looked around her. The soft light showed that she was lying at the bottom of a long slope covered with a thick carpet of bracken and heather which had served to break her fall. Yet they seemed to be in a cavern with no other entrance, than a dark, winding tunnel stretching away to their right.

"There, how does that feel?" Merlin sat back on his haunches as Rhea flexed her ankle cautiously

"Much better!" she replied with relief. "I should be able to walk on it now. Shall we go? The others must be worried." She held out her hand and the old man helped her to stand. The ankle ached abominably when she put her weight on it, but it felt no worse than sprained and Rhea could only be thankful she had escaped so lightly.

The tunnel stretched away in shadow, Merlin's light serving only to illuminate a few feet before them. Rhea felt her way along the walls, surprisingly smooth to the touch, as if polished by countless centuries of passage. The stone of the floor was worn into a deep furrow and sloped gently upwards, and, thought Rhea, into the heart of the mountain.

After perhaps ten minutes the wall beneath her hands disappeared and the passage opened out into a vast and beautiful cavern. Merlin's light danced on the glistening pillars and arches of the lofty hall, too faint to reach the roof, so that Rhea had no real idea of the dimensions of the space. She felt that it was immense and the echo of their footsteps seemed to come from a hundred directions at once.

"Welcome to the garden of Ogmios," said Merlin, his words echoing, whispered by ghostly voices till they faded into silence. "Here, outside of time, he tends the roots of the mountain and grows his home from living rock. Look well, Heart of Earth, for you will not see it's like again." Rhea was spellbound by the beauty of the place and could well believe that this spectacular hall had been wrought by art and not mere chance. All the colours of a pigeon's breast glowed on the graceful curves of the rock, catching and reflecting the golden witch-light.

Rhea had seen the show caves of Cheddar and the deep, silent caverns at Chislehurst, neither of which possessed the vibrancy and vigour of this place. Cheddar's wedding-cake loveliness was as nothing compared to the living filigree of stone through which she now walked.

In the centre of the cave, a large central space held a great slab of millstone grit, shaped like a couch with a raised pillar at one end. It reminded Rhea of the altar on the moor which she had touched that first day, save only that this was much larger and had not suffered the erosion of wind and rain.

"Ogmios' couch," Merlin explained. "Here he spends the centuries dreaming the shape of his garden and growing his crystals from seed." He indicated that she should look to her right and she saw a small field of crystal and semi-precious stones laid out in a spiral pattern on the floor. There were huge clusters of amethyst and quartz, glittering pyrites and all the varied hues of agate. One large stone, polished by the dripping moisture from the stalactites above, looked like black glass, frozen around a snowstorm. Rhea was bewitched by its soft sheen and reached out a hand to touch the surface.

"What is this, Merlin? I've never seen it before."

"The world calls it snowflake obsidian. You can see why."

"It is lovely."

"Ogmios would be pleased by your appreciation. He grew this as a memento of the first time he saw snow falling. It was at night, beneath a full moon at the dawn of life as we know it today. He thought it too beautiful to allow it to melt away forgotten so he caught the flakes in a stone the colour of midnight and preserved it for eternity.

"Geologists don't have all the answers," he chuckled. "They only understand the physical conditions required to produce these crystals. They will never understand that they were first dreamed to capture a moment of beauty which touched the soul of a grotesque giant whose very existence they would deny. Rose quartz was the light of the first dawn, amethyst the clouds of a summer sunset. Agates are all the colours of the autumn earth."

"And diamond?" asked Rhea, holding out the ancient ring on her finger, which seemed to have woken to life in this place.

"Starlight in frost," he smiled. Rhea nodded her understanding, humbled and grateful for the deeper understanding of the forces of the world that guided her. She had begun to see the life innate in her surroundings and with that privilege had come a renewal of wonder and respect.

"Come, child, the others will be worried, although Ogmios may have told them that you are safe." His face lit with unholy glee," In fact, if they have met my friend, they will probably be more concerned that they were before! This way!"

Merlin led Rhea through the scintillating garden of living rock towards a shadowy opening at the end of an avenue of slender columns ablaze with mica. Rhea turned before entering the tunnel to take one last look.

"I could never have imagined that so much beauty lay hidden in the earth beneath my feet. It feels right, though, somehow. I can feel the life in the stone. If I knew how to listen, I think I could hear them whispering all the secrets of the underworld." She turned away. Another unforgettable memory adding one more reason for her reverence of the earth upon which she walked.

A steep stairway, grown from the rock to fit the stride of Ogmios, wound upwards and inwards. Rhea found the going difficult, her ankle ached and the weight of the mountain above her was oppressive. They had been climbing steadily for perhaps two hundred feet when they hit a dead end.

"Sit down a moment, Rhea, and hold steady." said the mage. "Ogmios!" There was a terrific crash above their heads and the roof split asunder, showering them with earth and debris. Rhea raised her eyes, looking into a cloudless sky and the eyes of a giant.

Merlin clambered free of the hole and enormous hands reached down to lift Rhea to the surface. With great delicacy, a misplaced earthworm was removed from her hair, and then Anna and Jamie were hugging her. Rhea looked anxiously for Alec. He stood apart, head bowed and shoulders hunched, a position so uncharacteristic that she was alarmed. He rested on a sword like a battle weary gladiator, yet his whole bearing exuded defeat and despair. Rhea would have gone to him, but Merlin shook his head and motioned her to wait.

"Well met, old friend. It is long since you have visited my garden. It is good that you still walk the green earth."

"Well met indeed, Ogmios! We owe you thanks for your intervention. Surely our friend would have been lost without your help." Merlin drew Rhea forward to present her to the giant. "This lady bears the Sword of Earth."

Rhea looked up at the gnarled face above her. His eyes were deep and soft and meeting them Rhea forgot the twisted features, seeing only the beauty of the soul they reflected.

"May I thank you also for allowing me to see your garden? You have shown me loveliness where I never thought to look." The giant face broke into a crooked smile and he bowed low before her.

"Then, lady, all I have wrought is worthwhile. Earth-heart, give me your blade." Jamie returned the sword to Rhea, who laid it in the giant's outstretched hand. The Sword, dwarfed by the massive fist, yet retained an aura of power. "I read the signs in the earth and felt the blades awaken. A gift I give you, Light-wielder, to remind you of the beauty that is hidden."

Ogmios took something from the pouch at his waist and pressed it to the crosspiece of the sword. The metal glowed white-hot for a moment as the giant stroked the hilt and crooned over it. He bowed and handed the blade back to its keeper, beaming at Rhea's obvious delight as she examined his gift. Set into the hilt as if placed there at its forging was an oval stone. Rhea touched its glassy surface with tenderness as she named it.

"Snowflake obsidian."

Anna and Jamie came close to examine the stone and Ogmios turned his attention to Merlin. The giant gave him a brief account of the events above ground during his absence.

"The Windlord is troubled in heart, my friend. His grief overtook him and he would have harmed me, if he could, thinking me responsible for his loss. He feels that he is unworthy of his blade." Merlin looked pensive.

"This will have to be dealt with, and quickly. Will you stand with me, my friend?"

"As always, son of Cernunnos."

Merlin called to Alec, who straightened his back and approached them.

"Giant, I must apologise for my anger and beg your pardon. There is no excuse. I judged you by your appearance and my own fear. I am ashamed." He turned to Merlin, "I have let you down, you and the others. I think it would be better if I gave the Sword into safer hands."

"Alec, do you remember what I asked the other day? To admit your own weakness? You must learn from this. You have already recognised your error. Can you not see that you have already taken the first step towards wisdom?"

"Windlord, the Sword of Air was yours to win and yours to wield. If you walk away then all will fail. Is your shame greater than hope?"

Alec sighed.

"I am a fool, I suppose."

"Undoubtedly, love." Alec whipped around to find Rhea standing, arms akimbo, behind him. She led him a little apart from the others and they set their blades side by side on the short grass at their feet. Rhea held Alec's hands tightly as she spoke.

"... and when Anna told me what you had done, can you imagine how I felt?"

"I dread to think."

"Love, if anything were needed to convince me that the way we feel for each other is real and not some artificial emotion, born of these extraordinary days, then this evening would have given me all the proof I needed. When I was falling, beyond hope, my only thoughts were of losing you and Anna." Alec gripped her hands convulsively. "Yet, I was glad that even for such a short time, I had been given the chance to love you. It was a selfish feeling, if you think it through. There was no thought for our quest or even the feelings of those I would leave. But at the last, I am only human, with all the frailties and failings of my kind. Love came first with me too.

"That you should find the power to act as you did, that the Sword, a weapon of Light, should respond to your need, should tell you something. Is it wrong to feel and to love, to be human? Is that not why we were chosen as Champions?"

Rhea felt the tension begin to leave him as they sat together. On impulse Rhea picked up her blade.

"Take up your Sword, love. Ask for guidance." Alec carefully lifted the Sword of Air, weighing the blade in his hands.

"Who can I ask? Everything seems to have turned upside down."

"Does it matter what Name we call? Surely the One will hear whatever name we use." And together they sent out the call to the Lords of Light which is always answered when it comes from the heart.

Jamie and Anna had found comfort together. She had wept away fear and bound the long wound on Jamie's hand. They talked quietly of the evening's adventure and watched covertly as Rhea talked to Alec. They both heaved a sigh of relief when they saw them embrace. Alec would do now. Merlin was deep in conversation with Ogmios and the light had gone, leaving a vault of stars above.

"We will have to get going pretty soon," said Jamie. "It's a long walk to the nearest village, and I don't know how Merlin plans on getting us home. But I'm damned if I'll fly again tonight!" Anna gave a watery chuckle and asked, plaintively,

"Don't you trust me, Jamie?"

"When you haven't eaten since lunchtime? No!" The two grinned at each other. "Seriously, I wonder what the old man has in mind?"

"Come on," said Anna, grabbing his hand, "let's go and find out. I'm starving!" Jamie rolled his eyes in mock horror and followed her, grinning.

The four humans joined Merlin and Ogmios to discuss the next move.

"We need to get home and get some rest, I shall have to tend Rhea's ankle properly before bed and we can come at the next problem fresh tomorrow," the mage was saying.

"Jamie's hand is pretty bad too," added Anna. Jamie waved away their concern.

"Feeding Anna is my priority!" he laughed, dodging the blow she aimed at him.

"We're all too weary to consider night flying," Jamie beamed at this. "Now there are two swords to carry and two of us are injured. I suggest we walk down to Horton in Ribblesdale and call a taxi."

"I have a better idea. Sabrina was dining with Elizabeth tonight. If Jamie will call her on the mobile, she could pick us up. The way Bree drives, she'll be there in no time!"

"Okay, but it's a bad walk down in the dark. She'll be there long before us. Won't she?" This last, Jamie aimed at Merlin in deep suspicion. "No flying?"

"No flying, lad," chuckled the mage. "We'll walk. Will you forge the straight track for us, old friend?" Merlin asked the giant. Ogmios' eyes gleamed in the starlight.

"Willingly, son of Cernunnos. It is long since we walked such a path together. Stay close and have your children gather their courage." The giant walked to the centre of the plateau, caressing the earth and chanting softly. Merlin gathered the Champions and himself took up the rear, rekindling the golden orb which danced above his head. Slowly the ground melted away beneath the giant's hands, leaving a depression in the ground. Ogmios smiled at the company, and never breaking his chant, stepped into the hole, sinking into the rock as if it were quicksand.

"Follow the song, don't be afraid to breathe. I am behind you and you are perfectly safe," said Merlin.

Hand in hand Alec and Rhea stepped into the ground. Reality had been redefined so often over the past few days that they did not question Merlin's instructions. Jamie would have followed, but Anna hung back, horrified. The young man caught her hand and led her forward.

"Come on, I know this seems hard, but trust Merlin." Anna closed her eyes and stepped into the hollow. She felt herself sinking, down and down into some amorphous substance that was not the earth she knew. Terror welled inside. There was no solidity beneath her feet, no air, nothing but the weight of earth closing above her and the pressure of Jamie's hand. She dared not breathe. Seconds passed like hours as she fought back the screams. Her chest felt that it would explode. She had been buried alive.

"Breathe, Anna, you'll be okay. I don't know why or how, but it's okay." Jamie's voice brought her back and she instinctively gulped in a lungful of sweet air. "Now, open your eyes and look. It's amazing!"

Anna obeyed. The space through which they moved was filled with sparkling motes that danced to the giant's song. The air tasted clean and fresh as a spring morning with a warm afterglow of autumn. Ahead, Alec and Rhea were shrouded in dancing starlets of colour. Behind them, Merlin's witch light turned the air to gold.

Anna held out a hand. Tiny particles clustered around her fingers, clinging to invisible lines of force like iron filings round a magnet. Jamie, beside her, wore a nimbus of colour which pulsed and shimmered with every breath. Terror was forgotten as the company passed through the earth, following the song. Time had no meaning here, there was neither weight nor effort. Just a flowing. A strange, sleepy peace crept over them as they moved. They were aware that here was a life infinitely slower than their own but just as vital.

None could have said how long that journey lasted but eventually, the light changed, becoming harsh and cold and they felt the chill of stone beneath their feet. Merlin was bowing deeply before Ogmios in the moonlight.

"Thank you, old friend. I had almost forgotten that glory. It is good to be reminded." Merlin turned to his companions. "Never forget that you have travelled through the veins of the Earth. You have been carried in Her stream of life and breathed Her very essence. I do not think any other mortals have been so blessed."

Ogmios knelt before Anna, his eyes almost level with those of the young woman.

"Little sister, you have travelled through fear to faith. Remember me when all seems lost." He drew a small stone, the colour of living flame from his pouch and pressed it into Anna's hand. "Earthheart, come." Rhea's hand was lost in the grasp of the giant. "You have breathed the very lifeblood of Earth. She knows your name and will not forget. There is a bond and you will carry Her life within you as She carries yours. You will not forget." Rhea reached up and kissed the massive cheek, smiling. "Now, fare well, my friends and fare true." The giant laughed and disappeared into the darkness.

"Now, let's find that village and our lift home."

The village of Horton was asleep. Quiet lights glowed behind demure lace curtains and as the company waited in the main street there were few signs of life. Somewhere a baby cried, soon hushed by its mother; a dog barked in the distance, the soft laughter of lovers beneath the risen moon.

The roar of an engine shattered the peace as a car rounded the corner at high speed, screeching to a halt. The pulsing of drumbeats assailed the night as the door was flung open and a small, dark figure sprang from the driver's seat.

"Okay, would one of you gentlemen care to tell me what's going on?"

"Turn that dratted noise off, Bree! It's after midnight!" Alec strode forward, oblivious to the widened eyes of his sister as she saw the sword gleam in his hand. He reached into the car and switched off the ignition. "Come on, it'll be tight, but we'll manage."

Alec helped Rhea into the front seat, setting her ankle on his rolled up coat and stowing the two swords in the boot. Jamie and Anna squeezed into the back seat and Alec motioned for Sabrina to join them. "I'll drive, Bree, we've been terrorised enough for one night!"

Sabrina grinned, not having expected anything different.

"Where's the Professor? Mother said he'd be here too?" Merlin was nowhere to be seen. Something nudged Alec's ankle, and he quickly scooped it up and thrust it at his sister.

"Take this, don't ask and shut up. Sorry Bree, it's easier this way! I promise I'll explain later."

Confused and angry, Sabrina maintained a stony silence, all the way home, while the mysterious rabbit slept soundly on her lap.

Chapter Fifteen

THE BARD

There was a startling addition to the party in the study. Black skirts billowed out around the seated figure, heavy kohl outlined eyes set in a pale and lovely face. The dramatic effect, however, was somewhat spoiled by the mulish expression the little face was wearing.

"It's a wind up. You're doing it just to make fun of me," Sabrina glared at her brother. "You've always made fun of my beliefs!"

"No, Bree, honestly. It's all true. I've never understood your fascination with all this New Age stuff. Crystals, orbs and spirits and the rest. It's too much of a mish-mash to have made any sense to me. But I promise you, this is real and deadly serious."

"Prove it! No. You can't, can you?" She looked up at Merlin. "Professor, this has gone far enough. Tell me what's really going on here, please."

"It would be far better, child, if you had not become involved in this at all. But, as you have, you will just have to trust us. Many of the things you think you believe in have their roots in truth, older, deeper and far stranger than their modern shadows. You must learn to distinguish between the true and the false. Alec is right; this is no game but a serious and dangerous situation."

The lovely, petulant face regarded Merlin unconvinced, while the old man pondered how best to deal with the problem the child posed. They had given her the bare bones of the story, as factually as possible under such strange circumstances, but Sabrina refused to believe them, convinced that this was some elaborate practical joke.

"Oh, grow up, Sabrina-fair! Do you really think we'd all be in on this just for your benefit?" Jamie was finding the young woman very irritating. "What do we have to do to convince you?"

"Children, please!" Rhea stepped in, recognising the signs of a schoolyard squabble brewing between the youngsters. "Sabrina, dear, what would convince you that we are in earnest?"

"I don't know! I've never been faced with anything this crazy before! Even mother accepts your story, it seems, but all I get is told to shut up and given a rabbit to hold! What did you bring a rabbit for, anyway?"

Jamie's irrepressible good humour got the better of him and he winked at Merlin.

"Do you suppose we could explain that, Professor?"

"Oh, very well. I suppose it might serve. Sabrina, please watch carefully. Don't take your eyes off me for a second." The girl turned towards the fireplace where the Professor was standing and saw the air shimmer like a heat haze. Her jaw fell in astonishment as the familiar, rotund figure was replaced by that of a scruffy looking rabbit.

Anna, who had been observing quietly, thought how strange it was that the companions had all adjusted so quickly to these displays of arcane power. Except Jamie, she thought fondly, who still viewed them with delight.

Only Sabrina was left speechless as the rabbit shimmered first into the falcon shape, then back to Merlin's accustomed form. Incredulity, suspicion and wonder all chased across the girl's face in rapid succession.

"We couldn't all fit in the car, you know," said Merlin by way of apology. "And I was too tired to fly home."

"Well, what is my part in all of this?"

"I don't know. We are all taking the time on trust. It may be that you can remain safely on the side lines," Merlin explained.

"But I don't want to! That is real power, not the silly things my friends pretend they can do! I want to be a part of it!"

"Wanting is not enough, I'm afraid," said the mage kindly. "If there is a role for you in this, be sure it will find you in its own time. Then it will be time enough to choose."

"But if all you have told me is true, why can't you do something with all that power? What about hunger, disease, war... Why can't you just do something about all that suffering?" Alec caught Rhea's eye in quizzical recognition as his little sister went into her crusading mode.

"I'm afraid it is not that simple, child," said the mage. "Through hardship, pain and suffering each soul has the chance to make choices, to act and to learn. To grow. Happiness is wonderful! We couldn't survive without the little joys and simple beauty of life. They show us what the world could, and should be. But it is up to each of us to make it happen.

"There is a natural order to these things. Without hardship, how would we find courage? Without pain, would we know compassion? The small sacrifices of those who quietly tend the hearth fire and raise their families through difficult times, or the visible sacrifice of the soldier in battle, laying down his life for home, country and ideals. They are all one. They are made with love. They are the soul's response to the lessons we are offered. The choice belongs to every individual, and each time we choose Light over Darkness, it shines brighter within our hearts and lifts the darkness around us. It is a battle, or a glorious quest, every moment of our lives.

"The world is poised on the brink of the Age of Aquarius. The opposing forces of Light and Dark hold each other balanced, like a tug of war where both teams are absolutely equal. As the Aquarian Age dawns, the forces may lose that balance. There is a moment in time when we can wield the swords to preserve that fragile equilibrium and send out a note of pure harmony, like a cosmic tuning fork, that will set the 'tone' for the age to come.

"It will not eradicate evil, for night is as necessary as day. But it will, if we succeed, allow the next age of the world to begin at a higher octave, climbing to the next level on the spiral of life. The challenges faced, the sacrifices made, the choices of those who seek the Light on this journey will create a pattern, a blueprint, if you like, which will in turn be echoed in the hearts and minds of humanity for centuries to come."

Sabrina considered this in silence for a while. The quick mind was reflected in the mobile features as she struggled to come to terms with Merlin's answer. When she spoke, there was a new respect in her voice.

"So it's not that you can't or won't, it is that you shouldn't." Merlin nodded.

"Sometimes there are reasons that we, at our present stage of evolution cannot see or understand. Think of it this way; no mother wishes to see her child hurt, so she teaches him that fire is dangerous. Sometimes, she can tell the child over and over again to no avail. But let the child once burn his finger, and he will remember. Our higher selves know better than we what it is that we need and guide us towards understanding. In turn, they are governed by the forces of Creation themselves."

"What do you conceive as the purpose of all this, Merlin?"

"Alec, my dear friend, that is the hardest question of all!" the mage chuckled. "My own understanding is that we all carry a fragment, a tiny spark, of the great Source of all things, deep within us, like a central core of Light. We ... and I include all the manifested life forms of Creation... were made to allow those fragments to experience every aspect of life. To learn, to love, to sorrow and to laugh. To be born and to give life, to die and to close the eyes of a loved one. Over and over, in a great spiral of existence, until we finally return to the Light from whence we came. Rich with knowledge, understanding and wisdom, gained through our experiences and the choices we have made, and the Light Itself grows and evolves through our returning."

"'There is no part of me that is not of the gods'... I read that somewhere. I understand now, Merlin. I think part of me always did and that's why I've been diving into all the 'mumbo jumbo' as Alec calls it. Looking for this." Sabrina smiled up at the mage, her face alight with wonder. "If I can help, I will. If not, then I will wait till it is my turn." The smile turned to a grin of pure mischief. "Not that you are off the hook, mind. I shall have umpteen questions when I've digested this!" Merlin rolled his eyes in mock horror and the mood in the room lifted in response.

"I think my little sister just grew up," smiled Alec, bending down to give her a swift hug. "Now, Merlin, what's next?"

Rhea, however, felt uneasy and caught her daughter's eye. Something wordless passed between them as they recognised a hunger in the young woman.

"Sleep, I think! Some of us are getting on in years a tad, you know. It gets harder to stay up all night after the first millennium or so." Sabrina choked and immediately reverted to a little girl finding the fairies of her daydreams at the bottom of her garden, eyeing the ancient mage with awe. "Tomorrow we need to start looking for the location of the Sword of Water, I think."

"Well," said Rhea, who had listened in silence and at least agreed with Sabrina that this was what she had searched for all her life, "going on what we have so far, I'd imagine we need a waterfall, a river or a lake, don't you think?"

"Perhaps you could try and paint again, Mum?" asked Anna.

"Semer Water." All heads turned to Jamie, who was looking puzzled. "Don't ask me how I know that! But I'm certain of it. Semer Water." Merlin wrinkled his brows and the play of mixed emotions ran visibly through his face.

"Anything else, lad?"

"No, that's all. And I don't even know where that came from."

"Never mind, my boy, it will work itself out. Just take it on trust."

"How far is Semer Water?" asked Anna. The mage shook himself out of his reverie to reply,

"About thirty miles north west, as the eagle flies."

"We'll have none of that!" Jamie interjected. "Never again, if I can help it!" The mage shared a gleeful look with Anna.

"A little longer by road, I'd say. We'd need an early start. Tomorrow I think we need to rest a little, as it is tomorrow already," said Merlin, glancing at the clock. "We'll leave early the day after and make a day of it. Would you like to come with us, Sabrina? We can take two cars, so you don't have to hug a rabbit!"

The young lady stood and planted a cheeky kiss on the old man's face.

"I'd hug you anytime, old man!"

The old gentleman blushed.

Beside the spring in the oak grove a child lay sleeping. Born of Water and Light to meet the need of the quest. Soft tendrils of green-gold hair curled about her head, swaying in an unseen current. Her skin was pale and shone faintly as she stirred, gleaming like nacre. She woke as the starlight touched her face, stretching and rubbing the dreams from her eyes. Naked, she stepped into the pool in the shadow of the standing stone and disappeared below the silver surface of the water.

The morning dawned clear and bright, but only Jamie and Anna were awake early enough to appreciate it. Alec had taken Sabrina home with him at three and Rhea had stayed talking to Anna until almost dawn.

Merlin found the two young people in the study, poring over the legends of Semer Water.

"Afternoon, Merlin! How are you feeling? We've had a busy morning! The dogs took us for a long walk after breakfast, then we decided to see what we could find in here. No monsters are showing up, other than the usual fairies and boggarts that abound in all the old places." Anna smiled and waited for Jamie to finish speaking.

"I've just found this, though." She held out a much worn tome, open on a page illustrated with a line drawing of the lake. "There is a legend of a drowned city in the water." Merlin took the book and skimmed through the paragraphs that told the tale.

"Ah yes, I had forgotten about this! I've no idea how much truth there is to the story. There may have been a natural flood, of course. Sir William Watson, Burley's own poet, wrote 'The Ballad of Semmerwater' based on the legend, you know. There is usually something in the old tales that is true. Semer is a glacial lake, I believe, so it has been there longer than we have."

"What's the story, Merlin?" asked Jamie, gazing up from his cross-legged position on the floor, very like a small boy waiting for a treat. Merlin settled himself in an armchair, with the young people at his feet. For a moment he was taken back to the days of his youth when, as a Bard, he had taught the young Arthur the history of the land. Arthur was not unlike the young man at his feet, he mused. All fire and innocence, ablaze with life. When he spoke, his voice took on the cadence of the Bard of old and held his listeners spellbound.

"Long, long ago, when the world was still young, there stood a fair and prosperous city on the banks of a lake. The people were beautiful, dressed in fine linen and decked with silver wrought into delicate jewels. Their homes gleamed in the sunlight and there was music in the streets.

"One night, a poor and aged beggar stumbled into the town, cold, hungry and thirsty. He knocked on one fine door after another, only to be turned away by the haughty inhabitants. House after house closed their doors to him and sent him away unaided.

"At last, when he had tried every house, the old man found himself once more outside the great city. The sky was dark and clouded, with only the crescent moon to guide his steps. Some way ahead, the beggar saw a faint light and made his way towards it. The acrid tang of woodsmoke and tallow greeted him as he approached.

"The cottage was the merest hovel, a tiny building of wattle and daub, thatched with reeds. Outside a few chickens roosted and an elderly goat was tethered to a stake.

"The traveller knocked on the door and it was opened warily by a young man. When he saw the beggar was alone, he held the door wide and invited him into the warmth. Inside the cottage was clean and tidy, but very bare. A table of rough-hewn wood and two stools stood to one side, in the corner there was a curtained alcove with a rush mattress covered with a coarse, woollen blanket. On a stool beside the fire, a tired young woman sat spinning in the dim light. She looked up and smiled, laying aside the spindle with care and ushering the old man to her stool. She bade him sit and warm himself. Seeing him shiver, she took a large stone from the hearth, and, wrapping it in a fleece, placed it at his feet.

"The husband brought two beakers of ale and sat beside the old man and asked how far he had come and whither he was going, speaking to the beggar with kindness and respect. The young woman heated a soup of vegetables and herbs on the fire, placing cakes of bread to bake in the cinders. When all was ready, the meagre meal was shared with the old man.

"After they had eaten, the husband cleared a place near the fire for the old man to sleep, building up the sweet rushes and herbs and covering them with a blanket. Only when the beggar was comfortable did they blow out the tallow candles and retire themselves.

"The old beggar left the cottage while his poor but kindly hosts were sleeping. As he walked away, he looked down on the great, shining city below and said, "Semer water rise, and Semer water sink, and swallow the town all save this house, where they gave me food and drink."

"Next morning, when the young couple awoke, they looked for their erstwhile guest to no avail. Going outside, they saw that the once great city, and the valley where it lay, had disappeared completely and the waters of the lake now reached the edge of their little plot of land.

"Some tales say that the old beggar was really an angel in disguise. Be that as it may, no trace of the city or its inhabitants was ever seen again. But the stories tell that in times of peril one can hear the great bells booming in the deep water. I give you this tale from my heart to yours."

For a few moments longer, his little audience remained in attentive silence, savouring the magic of the Bard's voice. Listening to the old man, Jamie understood why the bards were so honoured in days gone by, when they trained for decades, learning their craft of voice and woven wisdom. It was Anna who broke the silence.

"Thank you, Merlin. That was a wonderful telling! I could see the place so clearly in my mind as you wove the tale for us! Funny, you know, we watch TV or read a story in a book, yet just listening to your voice really brought the tale to life for me."

"That, daughter, was the magic of the bards. Around the flickering flames of the home fires, they were given pride of place. Bringing news of the great happenings of the land, giving warning of invaders and battles, melding the isolated tribes into a nation through the power of their voices. Histories were taught, progress shared, teaching given and the flames of faith fed. Then, under the stars were told the age-old tales of the gods. Their audience spell-bound by the words of mystery.

"The training was hard and took many years. All the tales were passed from mouth to ear and learned by heart, so that each retelling was new and alive, animated by the soul of teller and listener alike. Is it not said that in the beginning was the Word? There is power in a voice and those the bards taught, heard with more than their ears alone."

Silence fell over the small room as the three returned to their perusal of the library. It was a peaceful scene, punctuated by the distant rattle of pans from the kitchen and the occasional quiet whimper from the sleeping dogs.

Nothing more of interest was found about the lake and it was decided that the party would leave early the following morning for Semer Water. They had nothing more than Jamie's certainty to lead them and the young man was a little concerned about this. Merlin, however, found nothing strange about the hunch, so Jamie decided that he would take it on trust and see what happened.

Later, alone in his bed, Jamie drifted between wakefulness and slumber. Fleeting visions, fragments of dream and memory, haunted his sleep.

He saw again the clearing in the oak wood and the pool by the standing stone. Stooping to drink, a face that was not his own was reflected there. A young girl with green-gold hair who smiled at him and held out her hand.

The vision faded, blurring into rainbows. In its place stood a fair city of tall, white houses and wide avenues. But the streets were deserted. No children ran and laughed in the sunshine, no maid drew water from the well and the market place stood empty. Jamie could hear his heart beating like the drumming of hooves and it was long before sleep took him into a white plain of mist.

Chapter Sixteen

SEMER WATER

The mid-morning sun had done little to chase away the mist wraiths that hung above the lake. Semer Water nestled grey and cold in its bleak dale. The companions gathered on the bank looked out as one across the silent mirror of the water. They had been here since dawn and had found no clue to the purpose of their presence. It was Jamie who voiced their thoughts,

"Now what?" The young man was acutely aware that the party was here on his instinct alone and felt helpless and uncomfortable. "Any ideas?"

"We're following you, lad." Merlin stared out across the lake. "Do you feel anything?"

"Only a bit of an idiot," said Jamie ruefully. He raked his hand through his hair. "I just know somehow that we have to be here. Or I thought I knew." Doubt flickered across his face and Anna squeezed his shoulder in reassurance. Jamie closed his eyes and tried to concentrate on locating the sword, drawing it to him as Rhea had done before.

"Where's that dratted brother of mine when you need him? We could use a nudge from Heilyn right now!" The old man stomped off and sat down on a large stone, muttering under his breath.

Alec turned away from the lake to scan the horizon, searching for clues. The tarn nestled between the Raydale hills. There were a few ruined buildings, small clumps of trees, but nothing stood out as a landmark.

A flash of white caught his eye, the only movement in the silent landscape. He watched in a desultory manner as a pretty white mare pawed the ground and shook her mane, while his mind searched for answers. Timidly the young mare came closer. Slowly, but surely she approached the party. Sabrina was at his elbow, watching entranced.

"She's the symbol of Epona, isn't she? The Horse Goddess in the Celtic myths."

"Of course. I never thought of that, I was miles away." Alec glanced at the blade in his hand. Sabrina laughed quietly.

"See, I told you I'd come in handy!" The young woman motioned to Jamie who came to stand beside her. The white mare was very close now. "Alec, look... she's not all there!" Jamie uncharacteristically bit back the retort that sprang to his lips, it seemed not the time for teasing. They followed her gaze and saw what she meant. "Look, you can see the hills through her flanks."

"Good Lord!" The exclamation drew all eyes to watch the final approach of the translucent, transcendent creature. Solid she seemed, white as carved ice reflecting rainbows of light. Gently she nuzzled Jamie and bent her foreleg before him, inviting the young man to mount. Jamie met the peat brown eyes of his mentor.

"Go on, lad. She's waiting for you."

Jamie took one deep breath and mounted, burying his hands in the snowy mane. The mare threw back her head, meeting the gaze of the companions, then walked towards the lake.

Stepping into the shallows her hooves seemed to melt away as the water lapped around them. Jamie took one last look behind him then set his face towards the centre of the lake as the deep water took them and he disappeared from sight.

Many things touched the calm acceptance that had suffused Jamie as he rode towards his destiny, but none broke through the barrier of conscious thought. He existed only in the moment, serenity incarnate. He felt detached, outside of reality and at peace with the rightness of his fate. As the waters closed over his head he did not fight.

On the bank, Alec held his sister as she watched, shocked to the heart, as Jamie sank into the depths. Merlin looked out across the water, searching with inner sight to see what was to come, but he could not pass the barrier of the shifting waters. All he could see was blood. From the deep, cold centre of the lake, a great bell tolled.

Jamie sank into darkness. He knew he should swim free and fight for the surface, yet he did not. The mare swam down, down, down into the depths and Jamie felt the pressure building in his lungs, burning with white fire. Tentacles grabbed at his hands and face, weighing him down, while the waters around him exploded into crimson.

Memory raked his heart. Rain lashing against the windscreen, thunder rolling in the hills. A flash of lighting illuminated the road as a great black horse reared in panic in front of the car. He heard his mother's cry as his father swore and wrenched at the wheel of the car. The screech of brakes and the scream of an injured horse. Then felt the second impact as the car hit the river. Water welling in through the doors, red with his mother's blood. She was silent now. There were no more screams.

The sticky black tentacles dragged him deeper. He watched again as his father fought to free him from his seatbelt. Heard that last command to take a deep breath. Felt one last time the hands that thrust him out through the window… saw once more the love and pain in his father's eyes before they vanished in the deep water.

Can you cry under water? Jamie did not know. But his heart exploded with grief and his world turned to night.

And yet still further. Down and down they took him. Down into the blackness of despair and loneliness. Down past the funeral, ebony and flowers and adults talking over his head. Lost child in a sea of amorphous faces. Down past the orphanage with its solitude and separateness. Down again through the succession of foster homes that could not cope with the grief-ridden child, locked in silence, down and down. And then, just as he knew he could take no more, just as he gave up, when all was black and hopeless, Jamie saw a golden gleam of love in a pair of peat brown eyes.

Darkness closed around him one last time and Jamie breathed a sigh of relief. His lungs filled with ice and he knew no more.

On the bank of the tarn the companions watched and waited. The wind had dropped and the water was still as the grave. Nothing stirred on the glassy surface yet the deep boom of a long vanished bell tolled mournfully.

Alec and Rhea stood side by side, gazing over the vast surface of the pool. In their hands the two swords carried their hope and love, channelling the will of the company out to their vanished friend. Merlin stood beside them, his head sunk low on his chest, with Anna in his arms. The old man had never felt so powerless. Doubt racked his mind, and fear for the boy. He could not bear another sacrifice, another young man riding willingly to seek his personal Grail.

Always before he had known, foresight had warned him, prophecy had guided him, necessity driven him. Yet here he stood and watched, simply a man, while the child of his heart rode out into the deep water alone.

Merlin thought back to the day he had first met the lad, tramping the moor alone. A scrubby little boy with a dirty, tear-stained face and defiant stare that had wrung the old man's heart. He had been sitting on a boulder, throwing pebbles into the stream and something about him caught the old man's attention. This was no place for a young lad alone in these times, yet there was no sign of anyone else on the moor that misty morning. He could feel the boy's distress tugging at his heartstrings, but he had kept his distance, shouting a greeting down the stream.

Jamie had wiped his nose on his sleeve before looking up. He had glanced around and seen the old man was alone except for old Jess, who had wagged her tail and wandered down to greet him at Merlin's silent prompting. The lad had stroked the black and white muzzle and Jess broke the ice as Merlin ambled down to the child.

He hadn't pried. He knew enough to understand the boy was hiding some deep hurt, so instead of asking the almost inevitable 'grown-up' questions, he had spoken to Jamie of the legends of the moors. The boy, at first defensive, warmed to the old gentleman, listening enthralled to the stories he wove and eventually accepting half a bar of chocolate Merlin had magically found in his pockets.

When he had stood up to leave, the old man suggested the two walk back together and Jamie acquiesced. Merlin could have watched over him by his own personal means, but by not asking questions, he had gained Jamie's trust.

As they reached the road, the old man had pointed out Stone Lodge and casually said the lad was welcome to stop by any time, as long as his family knew and approved. The boy's face closed down and Merlin had realised that here was the reason for the tears. A gentle push into the young mind elicited enough information for Merlin to find the boy again and they parted company.

The old man thought about the lad that evening as he sat before the fire and resolved to do what he could. He had always been a healer, and there was something about this boy that touched his heart. Something that reminded him of the first young man who had come into his care so many centuries before.

Careful enquiries found where the lad was living and Professor Ambrose met the foster family 'by accident' one day. Jess greeted Jamie as an old friend while the Professor chatted with the adults. Trading on his scholarly reputation in the village, Merlin praised the couple for the sterling job they were doing raising such an exceptional young man. He told them he had found the youngster bright and interested in the local legends and wondered if they would care to bring the lad round to Stone Lodge for tea one day, assuring them of Mrs Long's excellent cooking.

Giving the couple little chance to refuse, a date was arranged for the following Sunday afternoon before Merlin took his leave, winking at Jamie as the lad looked back and smiled. It was to be the first of many such visits.

That was ten years ago. The boy had grown into a man and, with Merlin's care, had learned how to smile and trust once more. The redoubtable Mrs Long had fed the child and extricated him from all manner of scrapes, patching torn trousers and plastering grazed knees while the Professor had fed the young mind. When Jamie had finally left the foster care system, it seemed a natural progression to continue his studies as the Professor's secretary, giving the young man a safe and loving haven from which to spread his wings.

Now, as he waited, fear took hold of Merlin's heart, feeling the echoes of distress from the lake, followed by the long, cold silence. The minutes ticked by like hours. No one spoke and the tension was palpable. Still the drowned bell boomed from the lake. One long knell after another, reverberating impossibly through the dale. Only when it stopped would Merlin cease to hope.

"Look!" It was Anna who first saw the point of light in the centre of the Lake. At first it seemed like a star dancing on the surface of the water. As it came nearer they saw with wonder that it was shining from the brow of the white mare, now revealed in her true glory. No longer young and timid, was she, but extravagantly beautiful, with a single, silver horn upon her brow.

She swam towards them, cleaving the water with her powerful neck, around which clung a limp figure. Behind Jamie rode a beautiful child with green gold hair, curling around her face in damp tendrils.

As soon as the unicorn touched her hooves to the lake bed, Alec was in the water. The watchers saw Jamie reach out and grasp his friend's hand and Merlin was flooded with relief.

Dripping rainbows as she walked, the unicorn carried her riders to the shore. Fully grown was she, her head held high and proud, carrying the silver horn like an affirmation. Sabrina thought she had never seen anything more beautiful and wished her mother was here to share the moment.

Alec helped Jamie to the ground. In his hand shone the third blade. It took only moments for the ancient mage to cover the ground and gather the son of his heart in a fierce hug.

Rhea was watching Jamie. Something had changed in the young face. Where before he had always hidden in laughter there was now a deep peace. He too had grown.

Handing the sword to Alec, Jamie turned to the little creature sitting silently on the unicorn's back. He looked up and smiled, holding out his arms for her to dismount, but she shook her head. Leaning down, she kissed the young man on the forehead, her face shining a pearl against the green-gold hair. Then the unicorn turned and silently carried its rider back into the lake.

The companions watched until the water that lapped gently around their feet closed over the two bright beings, and one small hand was raised in farewell.

Chapter Seventeen

NAMING LOVE

Three swords lay gleaming on the hearthrug, alive with the reflected flames of the fire that burned in the grate. The companions sat around the room, listening silently as Jamie told his story.

They had waited patiently until he was ready to share with them the experience beneath the surface of the tarn. He had been very quiet, driving home alone with Merlin in the second car while Alec and the girls had followed. They never knew what had been said between the two friends, but it had felt right to give them time to talk in private.

"... it was like waking into a nightmare within a dream. I could feel sticky limbs attaching themselves to me all over, leaching the life from me. When I dared to open my eyes, all I could see were these black things like huge worms writhing all around me. It was horrible." As he spoke, fear and disgust were etched on his face. "I was afraid. I tried to tear them off me, kick them away. The more I fought, the more I became entangled in them. I felt they would break me in pieces.

"I was about at the end of my strength. I don't know how long I had been fighting. A lifetime, it felt. Then I saw a glint of silver.

"I reached out, trying to move towards it, I hoped it was the sword. I thought of the old story of the Lady of the Lake and remembered Merlin. That made me smile inside. As soon as I smiled the tentacles seemed to flinch away. Then I heard a song.

"It was so beautiful that I was still and listened. I can't tell you how it lifted my heart. I just gave in to it and the black things began to melt away. It seemed as if I could fight the darkness all I liked, but I could never win. Yet, by surrendering to beauty and joy, the darkness could find no hold on me anymore.

"I closed my eyes and followed the song towards the point of light. I could feel the music drawing me and the tentacles released me. I drifted for a long time in a darkness that was soft, not menacing, with the melody all around me. I don't know how long. I suppose I must have been breathing, but it was no longer important. I just let the waters take me. After a while I could see light through my eyelids and I opened my eyes.

"I seemed to be drifting through a garden that swayed in the current. I followed a pathway of silver sand that led me over a hill. Beyond was a city of stark, white buildings. There was no-one there, so I followed the song. It led me down straight avenues bordered with flat roofed houses, I could see through the windows that the houses were ready for their occupants... tables were laid, toys were waiting for childish hands, tools lay awaiting their master, but there was no-one in sight.

"The paved roads ran straight towards the centre of the city. Beside the path were silent fountains and a stream that now lay empty. Every so often there was a crossroads, with a curving road either side. I felt the city was built in circles around a centre.

"After a while, I came to a great open space, paved and clean. It ran around the biggest building I had seen so far. Fish shoaled like flocks of birds above me. There were wide steps that led up to a columned façade, all made of some white stone with the sheen of polished marble. The roof gleamed a soft gold, casting rays of light into the darkness above.

"I climbed the steps and went inside. The hall was huge, echoing weirdly, almost like the sound in a swimming pool. There was a light, silver bright, shining against a dark doorway ahead of me. I seemed to be wading through water as I walked. I suppose I was, but it seemed the most natural element in the world.

"The room was lined with scrolls and books. All around the walls, millions of them it seemed. I got the impression that every human story was written and recorded here, every tear, every smile. The roof seemed to reach up beyond vision and the walls were not walls, but bookshelves, arranged in concentric circles around the brilliant glow in the centre.

"It took an age to get there. It felt as if I had been walking for years. Maybe I have. Time had a presence but no meaning. There was only now.

"She was there. The child, with her green-gold hair flowing out around her head as if caught in an unseen current. She was standing by a lectern in the centre of the space. The sword was in her hands and she smiled at me, holding out the blade."

Jamie glanced questioningly at Merlin.

"She called me Father and bade me take the blade. I asked her name and she shook her head, laughing. She told me she was born of water and Light and that her name was mine to give. She showed me a scroll on the lectern and gave me a pen made of a swan feather. Looking at her she radiated something so simple and beautiful, I could think of only one word. I named her Grá."

Merlin had tears in his eyes, but it was Anna who answered.

"Love. You named her Love."

Jamie nodded.

"It was as if I'd always known her, as if she was part of me, something small and fragile to cherish, yet as strong and keen as the blade in her hands." He shook his head slightly, as if trying to understand, trying to render the memory clear enough to grasp the elusive realisation that hovered around the edges of knowledge. "I took hold of the sword by the blade. It felt as if it bit deep into the flesh, painfully sharp. Yet there was no blood." He glanced down, rubbing his hands, expecting to see the white line of scars, yet knowing somehow that scars that were deeper than the skin had begun to heal.

"I had to kneel. The sword seemed to have the weight of the world in it. I marvelled at how she could have held it so lightly. She laughed again, and answered the thought as if she had read my mind. 'I am Love,' she said, 'I can carry anything.'

"Then she started to sing… so beautiful! I remembered the song I had followed through the fear. The song that had brought me to safety, and I realised that the singer and the song were the same, it was the melody of Love."

Tears welled in Jamie's eyes and trickled unheeded down his cheeks. Had he looked he would have seen them mirrored on the faces that watched him with the love of which he spoke. But he smiled, wonder lighting the boyish features.

"Then the white mare came back, only she shifted and grew, changing into that glorious creature you saw. The unicorn bent her head to the sword and touched it with her horn. I felt the power of it coursing through the blade and through my body. I don't understand it, but it felt like a blessing.

"Grá told me to mount and climbed up behind me. Such a tiny slip of a girl, yet she held me safe as the unicorn leapt into the space above the lectern and began a dizzying spiral, up and up. The tiny hands holding me just felt like coming home, somehow.

"I'm not sure if I lost consciousness, or fell asleep, but I saw my parents, holding hands and smiling at me." A sob caught his throat, but his face was suffused with tender joy. "It was beautiful."

Silence held the room for a long moment, a silence filled with such warmth and love that wrapped itself around the young man, healing a heart broken too early and never wholly mended. Anna reached out and placed her hand in his, wordless understanding passing between them in a heartbeat.

"Then she brought me back. She brought me home."

Chapter Eighteen

WOODHOUSE CRAG

The morning had dawned grey and drizzly, incongruously dismal after the events of the preceding day. The company had gone about its daily business in a desultory manner, unable to reconcile the wonder of the quest with the mundane necessities of normality.

Merlin brooded in the library all day, poring over ancient tomes, searching for clues he knew he would not find, reluctant to cease the search and fall back into worry for the people he loved. Every so often he glanced at the clock, waiting for the hour when they had agreed to gather for dinner. The day passed slowly, dragging its feet as his disquiet grew.

He smiled as he heard Alec's car pull onto the gravel. A glance through the window showed the light still on in the studio. Just the youngsters now and they had gone wandering the moors together. Dusk was fast approaching and the savoury aroma emanating from the kitchen heralded dinner.

The old man was settling into comfort, chuckling at an old tale in a dusty volume, when the telephone shrilled, making him jump and dive for the handset. A rapid exchange and he was on his feet, gathering the swords left in his care, with purpose and urgency in every line of his body.

He grabbed a coat from the rack in the hall, bundling the blades unceremoniously into another as Mrs Long appeared in the doorway. That redoubtable lady stood arms akimbo, barring the way, looking at the ancient mage with that indulgent and long suffering resignation common to all mothers of small children. The Keeper of Light for the Age shuffled his feet uncomfortably, feeling like a five year old caught in mischief.

"Tha' knaws that t' dinner's nearly done?" Merlin nodded, feeling as if he'd been found dismembering a butterfly. "An' I suppose tha's going ter ask me to keep it warm. And tha's not bahn to tell me what tha's up to?" It didn't seem worth risking a response in face of her stern certainty. "An' in all these years tha's nivver given a thowt to t' fact Ah've got eyes in me 'ead and a good pair of ears either side?

"Away with ye, ye daft old beggar. Look after them children, Mr Merlin. There'll be food in t'range when tha brings 'em 'ome."

She propelled the astonished mage out of the door, closing it behind him and leaving him speechless on his own doorstep. The martial strains of "Fight the good fight" receded into the distance as he wondered just how much the old lady knew.

Filing his rueful wonder for later consideration, he crossed the yard swiftly, meeting Alec and Rhea at the studio door. Their expressions told him they already knew something was afoot and little discussion was needed as the three piled into the car turning right out of the gate onto the road that skirted the moor.

It was only a matter of ten minutes to reach Heber's Ghyll. They parked the car and headed up the path than ran beside the tumbling waters. Once deep in the cover of the trees Merlin called a halt. The three swords were unwrapped, Alec and Rhea taking theirs with that strange electric reverence running through them and placing them on the ground at their feet.

"Jamie's call said we needed to get there fast. Woodhouse Crag is a good way from here, as you know, Alec. Hold tight and hope no one sees us. The swords will help…"

There was no preamble as their shapes shimmered and melted. Rhea felt herself change, her senses becoming keener, catching a vague scent of fire and fear in the wind. And something familiar. Her feet felt deeply attuned to the earth and she looked in joy at the two wolves that stood before her.

Wordless communication surged between them and she wanted to howl in sheer delight at the rising moon, just visible through the treetops. But she understood the need for silence, could smell the fear. She picked up the sword between her teeth, relishing the strength in her jaws, loving the feeling of power in her frame.

A shared glance and the three were off, running like the wind up the steep path, out onto the moor by the bridge and right along the edge over the stiles that punctuated the dry stone walls.

Sheep scattered in panic as they ran. The valley spread out beneath them, beginning to fill with coloured stars as cars and houses lit their lamps against the encroaching darkness. To their left the high moors stretched away into darkness, lit only by the faint moonlight reflecting through the roiling clouds.

The sharp tang of burning grew as they ran. They were headed for the Swastika Stone.

Rhea had never seen it but the ancient carving had made its presence felt in the trinket Anna had given her. It was a place of eldritch power, she knew, the great carved boulder clinging to the edge of the crag, brooding the secrets of solar fire. Of course… fire. The final piece of the jigsaw.

The vulpine forms shifted back to their own as they ran. It was Alec who cried out, seeing a dark form limned in crimson and suspended above the rock. The deep orange glow flickered against the blackness. Two figures clung to each other, silhouetted against the flame, desperation in every line, their eyes fixed on the apparition before them.

Rhea ran to her daughter, taking the weeping form from Jamie's grasp as the young man lurched forward to restrain Alec.

Her face stretched in a rictus of pain and terror, it was Sabrina who hung in the flames. In her hands the fourth sword burned incandescent. The long black hair flew about her head as if caught in some diabolical breeze. Alec broke free of Jamie and threw himself into the flame but was thrown back, the smell of singed hair and flesh rank in the night.

In a strange pool of silence Merlin took in the details of the scene. That moment outside of time felt weary, full of pain and sorrow. He wondered how much one heart can bear before it breaks. Centuries of old heartache threatened to engulf him in grief as he watched the young life burning away before his very eyes. Age and doubt crept over him and he felt spent and powerless. But only for a second. Less than a second. He took a deep breath…

Yet it was Rhea who broke the stasis that seemed to hold them all. Dragging her sobbing daughter to her feet she slapped her face, once. The sound drew all eyes as Anna gasped in shock.

"That's better. Now, Anna. Bearer of Flame. Take up your blade."

The girl looked at her mother as if she were a stranger. Indeed Rhea's bearing was no longer that of an uncertain housewife but regal. Strength personified. Anna simply nodded and turned, walking towards Sabrina in her lambent prison.

Those few steps seemed to take forever to the young woman. Scenes of other days, of childish laughter, a father's smile and her mother's arms superimposed themselves on her eyes. The heat of the flames became the warmth of summer days beside the sea, and her heart filled with love and memory as she walked. She could feel the cool water of the rock pools where they had searched for crabs and anemones, the salt spray on her lips that tasted like tears. She climbed the rocks with echoes of laughter in her ears and the silent scream of the girl before her became the cry of the seagulls in the blue summer sky. Anna smiled and reached out her hands.

Rhea stood alone, as straight as the blade she carried and watched her daughter walk into the flames. She could not see those images of childhood, but she saw others. She once again watched her daughter step into a new life. For this was a birthing in many ways. With the fourth blade something new would come into being and Anna was both child and midwife to the birth.

Rhea refused fear, turning her back on it resolutely and accepting only faith and trust in the Purpose she served, feeling only tenderness and pride as Anna stretched out her hands and took the blade amid the inferno.

There was a moment when the flames warred red and gold, raging against the night sky, flaring like the beating wings of a dragon. Then the gold flickered and grew, subsuming the scarlet, gentling it, consuming it in quietness.

Merlin and Rhea watched the young men run to catch Sabrina as she fell. Alec reached her first and lifted the limp form like a rag doll, cradling his little sister to his chest.

The old mage felt withdrawn, somehow, and saw a similar story written on Rhea's face. But while he felt almost outside of the scene, she was more present than the moment itself. All the human emotion was there, the love and pain, the fear and pride. Yet there was something else in her eyes. Something extreme and absolute in the clarity that he recognised, a serenity as she turned and smiled at him in simple joy. He had seen that look before. Those were the clear eyes of purpose that he had seen only once or twice in his long life. Yet as he watched they were met and mirrored by those of her daughter. This was the power of the Mother and he remembered the ring that she wore and bowed his head, humbled before their combined Light.

It was only an instant. A moment of grace outside of time. Then all were crowding round the limp figure Alec had laid on the heather.

Jamie took his sword from the mage and smote the earth. He understood these things somehow. He felt the earth and the water that was its lifeblood flowing through it and from his knowing water welled from the ground, bathing the seared body in a cool spring as Merlin knelt beside her and sent his healing senses through her flesh.

Tears streamed down Alec's face as he bent to catch a whispered apology from the scorched lips. She struggled to form the words as he tried to hush her. Pride had brought her here, second-guessing their intent, a desire to *do* rather than simply be. She had called the sword, knowing it was waiting, half formed for the call, and it had come. Held in the claw of a winged serpent of flame and she had grasped it, caught by the glamour of power. And it consumed her.

Jamie and Anna had found her there and raised the alarm when they could not reach her. Fear had held them back, a barrier as lethal as the flames. Only the severity of Rhea's intervention had brought Anna to the calm from whence she could act.

Rhea nodded to her daughter, aeons of knowing passing between the two pairs of eyes. Then she too sent out a call. And it was answered.

The hilltop began to fill with presences seen and unseen, half glimpsed in the moonlight, encircling the companions in a throng that spanned the worlds.

Chapter Nineteen

SWORDS OF DESTINY

Merlin looked up from his task as the presences crowded in around them, weighing on his consciousness. He alone recognised the majority of those who attended this birth in Light. Faces from the past, Champions of Light long faded from the world. Legends and friends.

But some were familiar to all. The crowd parted to allow Cernunnos and Mab to enter the circle, bowing to the Forest Lord and the Lady of the Fae.

He saw in astonishment that Heilyn had not arrived alone, but led Elizabeth by the hand, bringing her to her daughter. The graceful figure laid her hand on her son's shoulder, smiling gently with a serenity that echoed that in the eyes of Rhea and Anna…Maiden, Mother and Crone, thought the mage. He had not Seen.

Alec stood to allow his mother to take his place. The waters of Jamie's spring washed the hurt and charring from Sabrina's face like gentle fingers, smoothing away the pain as life ebbed away from her. And there were hands in the water, Alec realised, and a face he remembered, as Verbeia swirled into being, taking the damaged girl in her arms and laying her head amongst the flowing rainbows of her gown.

"I will take her and heal her. I will take her back into birth and renewal and she will learn the ways of Water to balance the Flame." The silvery voice spoke softly to Elizabeth, who nodded her willingness. She had known, always known, the wildness in her daughter, the pride and hunger that were a misguided search for meaning. She kissed her daughter one last time and watched in love and grief as the form which had grown within her own flowed like water into the earth, leaving no more than a trace of starlit dew on the grass that accepted the tears that fell from her eyes.

A silent tension spiralled around them that to Merlin's other senses seemed like a vortex beginning to build.

"It is time, my son," said the Horned One. For once, however, Merlin was at a loss. He had brought them this far, but could not see what was to come. He looked helplessly at his protégées.

"Not all things are in your control, child," said Mab, "Not all are your responsibility or yours to hold. Stand back from this. You have done your part. For now." She smiled, not unkindly, yet there was still a glint of knowing mischief in her eyes.

The four sword bearers stood at the centre of the circling force, a silent eye of calm at the heart of a storm, it seemed, while the mage struggled to assume this unaccustomed role. He need not have worried, he realised, they knew what was required, so in tune were they with each other and the Purpose that guided them.

Rhea held her blade aloft and the others followed her lead, the points of the swords forming a pyramid in the central space that seemed to his inner sight to send up a fountain of liquid Light that fell to earth and flowed out across the landscape.

Slowly, softly as a sunrise over the misty moorlands, a figure began to take shape within the glow. Merlin could feel the changes, but could not grasp their meaning. A strange confusion came over him, an excitement, wholly human and long forgotten. Recognition. Priestess of the Mother who had once worn a red-gold ring. He felt the flush of yearning as the figure held up a vessel filled with Light. Cernunnos bowed his horns and the gathered company followed his lead. All except one.

Tonight she was not blind. Tonight she saw clearer than the rest, straight into the heart of love and life, beyond the ages, beyond fear, beyond hope.

Elizabeth saw the elemental powers playing around the blades. She saw that they were not four but One, symbols of a unity refracted in manifestation. Perfect only when whole, united. She watched as the young ones drew in that balance and sent it spinning through the worlds, confident in joy and pain, accepting and assuming Love and loss, annealing pain.

But there was one loss that did not have to be on this night of power.

Not again. Not tonight.

To Rhea. the Earth felt alive in her as a growing child. She felt its heart beating in harmony with her own and sent out her mind and love, feeling her way through soil and stone, tree and leaf. She felt the life of the earth in her own veins, the song of birds, fur and scale, the scurrying of insects and the exuberance of burgeoning life. She could not heal it all alone, but she felt the others with her, each bringing an equal part. Their magic would not make it whole, would not heal all the hurts, but it was enough. It was possibility. It was a seed for growth.

Elizabeth smiled at Rhea, sharing a moment's knowing, heart to heart and eye to eye, then laid a hand against her son's wet cheek. She stepped into the glow with the misty figure and raised her hands for the Cup.

No-one heard the words that passed between Elizabeth and the shining being, if indeed any were spoken, but she took the vessel and held it aloft, taking the place of she who had come. Radiating peace and beauty like a benediction, she smiled at her son in farewell as the light faded and Elizabeth gave herself into Its service.

A voice whispered from the fading glow,

"My beloved children, *you* are the Swords."

Then she was gone and the hilltop sank into darkness.

It was Anna who lit the night. The Swords were no more, taken back to whence they came. Yet their power remained. They were the swords. Each of them could feel the power of their own blade within, echoed and harmonised by the others. They had become that which they had sought and borne and the magic ran through them. The flame of her witchlight danced on Anna's hands and lit the hilltop.

She send it fluttering like a butterfly, past her mother and Alec, hand in hand, riding the Windlord's breeze, past Jamie whose tears caught the faint light like his smile as he marvelled at the clear water welling from his hands, to where the Keeper of Light faced an impossibility.

There was one loss that did not have to be. Not tonight. Not again. There would be grief, there would be tears. But for now, joy too was allowed. The magnitude and beauty of Elizabeth's gift was made clear with a single, incredulous word from the mage.

"Nimue!"

EPILOGUE

Merlin gazed in wonder at the golden head on his lap. Older, she was, than when he had first heard her silver laughter, younger than when he had lost her to time. She would not speak of the centuries of service. She merely smiled, and that was enough.

Through the open door of the library he could see the Champions sitting at the table, talking quietly. There had been grief and tears and only time would heal their human hearts. But there was understanding too, of sacrifice and the love that inspired it. There was change, in the four who were now Keepers of Light, who had grown through fear and courage and lived with a vibrancy that sang in the heart of the mage and echoed through the worlds, a quiet seed of hope for a new aeon.

Jamie, delighting in the watery magic in his fingertips, poured miniature waterfalls from one hand to another. Anna laughed, the sound of a passionate joy,

"Oh, you *boy*!"

The mage met the smiling eyes of his love in silent happiness.

There was beauty in the world tonight.

ABOUT THE AUTHOR

Sue Vincent is a Yorkshire born writer, who has been immersed in the Mysteries all her life. She is a teacher and Director of The Silent Eye, a modern Mystery School. Sue co-authored *The Mystical Hexagram* with Dr G. M. Vasey and many other books, both alone and with her co-Director, Stuart France.

The writing partnership of France and Vincent has a peculiar alchemy of humour, scholarship and vision that has given birth to many books, including the The Triad of Albion, Doomsday and Lands of Exile series'.

Sue has a lasting love-affair with the landscape of Albion, the hidden country of the heart. She lives in Buckinghamshire, having been stranded there some years ago due to an accident with a blindfold, a pin and a map. She is currently owned by a small dog who also blogs.

You can follow their adventures online at scvincent.com or franceandvincent.com and find Sue on Twitter @SCVincent.

IF YOU HAVE ENJOYED THIS BOOK,
PLEASE CONSIDER LEAVING A REVIEW ON AMAZON OR GOODREADS.

THE SILENT EYE

The Silent Eye School of Consciousness is a modern Mystery School that celebrates the inherent magic in living and being. With students around the world, the School offers a fully supervised and practical correspondence course that explores the self through guided inner journeys and daily exercises.

The Silent Eye also offers regular workshops that combine ritual, talks and informal gatherings within the landscape, bringing the teachings to life in a vivid and exciting format.

The Silent Eye operates on a not-for-profit basis. Full details of the School, the distance learning course and upcoming events may be found on the official website: www.thesilenteye.co.uk.

Books by Sue Vincent

THE OSIRIAD
MYTHS OF ANCIENT EGYPT

"There was a time we did not walk the earth. A time when our nascent essence flowed, undifferentiated, in the Source of Being."

In forgotten ages, the stories tell, the gods lived and ruled amongst men. Stories woven of love and loss, magic and mystery, life and death. One such tale has survived from the most distant times. In the Two Lands of Ancient Egypt a mythical history has been preserved across millennia. It begins with the dawn of Creation itself and spans one of the greatest stories ever to capture the heart and imagination.

In this retelling of the myths of Ancient Egypt, it is the Mistress of all Magic herself who tells the tale of the sacred family of Egypt.

"We have borne many names and many faces, my family and I. All races have called us after their own fashion and we live their stories for them, bringing to life the Universal Laws and Man's own innermost heart. We have laughed and loved, taught and suffered, sharing the emotions that give richness to life. But for now, I will share a chapter of my family's story. One that has survived intact through the millennia, known and remembered still, across your world. Carved in stone, written on papyrus, I will tell you of a time when my name was Isis."

STUART FRANCE AND SUE VINCENT

TRIAD OF ALBION
THE INITIATE ~ HEART OF ALBION ~ GIANTS DANCE

Don and Wen thought it was just a day out in an ancient landscape wrought in earth and stone, walking the sacred ways of the Old Ones. They could not know what mysteries would unfold as the birds led them deep into the legendary history of Albion.

As the veils thin and waver, time shifts and the present is peopled with shadowy figures from the past, weaving their tales through a quest for understanding and opening wide the doors of perception for those who seek to see beyond the surface of reality...

DOOMSDAY
THE ÆTHELING THING,~ DARK SAGE ~ SCIONS OF ALBION

What exactly were the Norse gods doing on a supposedly Christian artefact that looked more like a standing stone than a cross? Don is drawn to investigate, questioning the history of the Blessed Isles of Albion, while Wen determines to restore the position of one particular stone. Which would have been alright if Ben hadn't gone back for the gun…

LANDS OF EXILE
BUT 'N' BEN ~ BECK 'N CALL

While Ben, fast becoming a folk her, languishes in Bakewell Gaol, Don and Wen are on holiday… or 'on the run' if Bark Jaw Dark and PC 963 Kraas, hot in pursuit, are to be believed.

From England to Scotland and Ireland, the officers of the Law follow the trail of the erratic couple.

But who is the shadowy figure, hovering beyond sight?

What is his interest in a small standing stone and just how many high-level strings can he pull… and why?

OTHER BOOKS BY SUE VINCENT

Loreweavers

An Imperious Impulse: Coyote Tales

WITH DR G. MICHAEL VASEY
The Mystical Hexagram: The Seven Inner Stars of Power

BOOKS BY STUART FRANCE

The Living One: Contemplations on the Gospel of Thomas

Crucible of the Sun: The Mabinogion Retold

Pieces of Nietzsche: A Thinker's Bias

Slivers of Søren: Testaments to Truth

AVAILABLE VIA AMAZON WORLDWIDE